OSLg

D1263549

THE ELUSIVE CONSULTANT

BY
CAROL MARINELLI

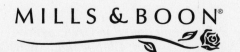
MILLS & BOON®

For Anne, Tony, James and Hannah
with lots of love.

*First published in Great Britain 2003
Large Print edition 2004
Harlequin Mills & Boon Limited,
Eton House, 18-24 Paradise Road,
Richmond, Surrey TW9 1SR*

© Carol Marinelli 2003

ISBN 0 263 18140 5

*Set in Times Roman 17 on 18½ pt.
17-0304-48598*

*Printed and bound in Great Britain
by Antony Rowe Ltd, Chippenham, Wiltshire*

CHAPTER ONE

'I HEAR Max is leaving us.'

'Apparently so.' With her usual smile still in place, Tessa paid for her meal and waited while Narelle, the canteen lady, swapped over the coffee-jugs.

'The place won't be the same without him—doctors like Max don't come by every day. He saved my Bruce, you know.'

Tessa did know!

Not only had she been on duty the day Narelle's husband had been wheeled into the department in full cardiac arrest, she was made to relive the moment in glorious Technicolor every morning when Narelle fussed over her like a broody hen, forcing food on her as some sort of bizarre reward and doing unmentionable things to Tessa's calorie count. 'Dead as a dodo he was, and just look at him now, and it's all thanks to

5

Max, and you, of course. I'd best go and put his eggs on. You go and sit down, love, and I'll bring your meal over. So who's going to be your brunch buddy now?'

Who indeed?

Sitting at her usual table by the window, Tessa stared at the glistening bay, curling her heavy chocolate curls idly around her fingers as she drank in the view she never tired of. The water so still and calm, it looked as smooth as glass, reflecting the sun high in the late morning sky. But as idyllic as it all looked, the postcard scene was marred by the sight of a red helicopter whirring in the distance, buzzing on the horizon like an angry bee. The water might look calm, but looks were deceptive and Tessa knew that only too well.

The dangers of the ocean were rammed home with alarming regularity at Peninsula Hospital. A bush hospital they might be, but what they 'missed' in stabbings and drug-related problems, they made up for tenfold with a never-ending stream of multi-traumas, courtesy of Mother Nature. Frowning slightly, Tessa screwed up her eyes, trying to pick up any obvious problems, anything that might indicate what the rescue helicopter was doing out at this time. Tessa knew their schedule almost as well as she knew the emergency department's, and a training run at eleven-thirty wasn't their usual practice. Hopefully, she'd asked for her eggs runny. If the emergency chopper was out on rescue, no doubt she'd be being summoned in the not-too-distant future!

Oh, well, she'd find out what it was all about soon enough, Tessa thought with a shrug, adding half a sachet of sweetener to her black coffee before gingerly taking a sip.

It tasted awful but, Tessa thought with a sigh as she forced herself to drink it, maybe she was being a bit harsh, blaming the coffee. After all, nothing was going to taste particularly sweet this morning with the bitter taste Tessa had in her mouth.

Max is leaving.

It was all she had heard all morning. A cruel game of Chinese whispers whizzing through the emergency department. Each version just a little bit different, a touch more exaggerated perhaps, but it all boiled down to the same thing.

Max really was going and he hadn't even thought to tell her.

OK, they weren't *best* friends, they didn't ring each other every evening to gossip about the department and, apart from work dos and the endless breaks they whiled away together in the hospital canteen, their friendship didn't equate to the outside world. They'd never shared a dinner or even so much as a coffee that hadn't been made by Narelle.

But Tessa had always thought they were more than just colleagues. Nine times out of ten Max joined her for brunch and a gossip, invariably he would tap her on the shoulder if he needed help with a patient and they often whiled away the lulls in Emergency over a coffee and a chat. He knew every last one of her dating disasters, and in turn Tessa knew all about his fiancée Emily and her eternal quest to 'fix a date.' They *were* more than just colleagues and the fact Max had sat on the biggest piece of news since the turn of the century hurt.

Really hurt.

'Why the miserable face?'

So deep was Tessa in her thoughts she hadn't even heard Max approach, and by the time she looked up he was already pulling up a chair and sitting down, wearing his usual shorts and T-shirt, coupled with his trademark wide, easy smile.

Grateful for the excuse, Tessa replaced her cup in her saucer and grimaced. 'Despite what the label says, this tastes nothing like sugar.'

'You're not on another diet?' Max groaned. 'If it's that cabbage soup one, I'm really going to have to put my foot down. Every time you pulled out that Thermos I felt like ducking for cover, I couldn't stand the smell.'

'Me neither.' Tess laughed. 'And, no, it's not the cabbage diet and it's not the milk-shake one either—this one involves real food and lots of it. Narelle's cooking up a storm back there.'

'So how was the course?'

'Great.' Tessa gave an enthusiastic nod. 'I learnt heaps, which is just as well, Admin were very reluctant to fund it. You'd have thought I was asking them to pay me for a week by a pool in Queensland, not an advanced trauma course.'

'That's so like them,' Max groaned. 'You'd think the money came from their own wages sometimes.'

'They only agreed in the end because I had my own accommodation lined up.' Tessa grinned. 'Hotel Hardy.'

'How was it?'

'Oh, the food was wonderful, the service amazing and the bedroom divine. There's nothing quite like your old bedroom, is there?'

'How's your mum?' Max asked, his laughter fading as he watched Tessa stiffen.

'Oh, fine,' Tessa said airily, then, feeling the weight of his stare still on her, she gave a little shrug. 'She's still living in la-la denial land.'

'Thing's haven't got better, then?' Max asked gently as Tessa shifted uncomfortably.

'Dad's back with *her.*'

'His mistress?' Max checked.

Tessa gave a low laugh. 'Whatever you want to call her.'

'Maybe he isn't back with her this time, Tessa, maybe it's all innocent. You might just be reading too much into things.'

'No, I'm not.' Her voice was sharp, her eyes defiant as she looked up. 'I know I'm right, the same way I've always know since I was ten years old. The pattern's been the same—later and later back from the office, more trips to Sydney than a flight attendant, and endless presents for Mum to quash his guilt. The front room looks like a funeral parlour there's so many flowers in there. I don't know how Mum can let him get away with it, and as for her…' Tessa's full mouth practically disappeared into her face as she sucked in her cheeks. 'How could she do it? Leaving aside how many people she's hurt over the years, how can she bear just to have a part of him?'

Max didn't say anything, just watched as she leant back in her chair and nibbled at the skin around her thumbnail, her serious brown eyes finally coming back to meet his. 'Mum just refuses to believe it, she just can't see that it's all happening again.'

For an age he didn't answer, just stared at Tessa thoughtfully. 'That's her prerogative, Tessa,' Max said slowly. 'Maybe she knows exactly what's going on and just chooses to ignore it. The truth hurts sometimes.

'Anyway, enough about grown-up games, let's get on to brighter things.' He gave her the benefit of a very nice smile and Tessa gave a grateful sigh as Max sensibly moved the subject to safer ground. 'I missed you while you were away.'

The grateful sigh caught in Tessa's throat. Max saying he had missed her definitely wasn't safer ground. Max saying he had missed her sent her imaginations soaring, and her heart fluttering, so for something to do Tessa's thumb went up for a second nibble. 'Don't you mean you miss the way I do your bloods and generally clean up behind you?' Tessa said, forcing a half-laugh, trying to keep the conversation light.

'No, Tessa, I missed *you*.'

Wrong answer.

An imaginary gong sounded in Tessa's head and she could almost hear the clock ticking as she struggled to come up with a witty reply, a quick bucket of water to douse the undercurrents that were sizzling across the table. What the hell was going on? Max never spoke like this, never leant across the table with puppy-dog eyes and nervous smiles. He'd only said that he'd missed her, Tessa frantically reasoned, but it wasn't so much what he'd said but *how* he'd said it. Not once in their five-year history had there been any subtle connotations, any shifts in tempo, but all of a sudden here Max was telling her he'd missed her, with eyes that seemed to be directed to her very soul.

'The chopper's out,' Tessa said in a flurry of nervousness, gesturing to the window and wishing she could rest her burning cheeks against the cool glass. 'I can't see anything going on, but it isn't their usual time for a practice run.'

The tension that had built around them popped like an overblown balloon as Max turned his attention to the window. 'It isn't a practice, they just called for a doctor assist.'

Tessa heard the edge in his voice and found herself smiling. Max lived for call-outs, unlike Tessa whose blood ran cold each and every time she was summoned to the chopper. 'So how come you're not out with them?'

'It's Chris Burgess's turn this week, lucky thing. I haven't been out to a good rescue for ages.'

'We were out there two weeks ago,' Tessa pointed out. 'I've still got the vertigo to prove it. I don't know how you can get such a kick out of it.'

'Tessa Hardy, you know you love it really,' he teased, but Tessa shook her head adamantly.

'Solid ground does it for me every time. I freeze inside when they ask for a nurse assist. It's not the patients that worry me. I enjoy a good multi-trauma just as much as you, Max, and I love going out with the road ambulance, but helicopters...' Tessa gave a small shudder. 'If I never set foot in one again it will be too soon.' Her gaze drifted back to the window. The helicopter was long since out of sight, the perfect scene uninterrupted now. 'It's hard to believe someone might be in trouble out there when it all looks so picture perfect.'

'Isn't it just?'

Something in his voice dragged Tessa's attention away from the view, a distant pensive note that sounded so, so out of place with Max's usual easygoing manner.

'I guess things aren't always as idyllic as they seem,' he said slowly, the dark note to his voice so audible Tessa felt the hairs stand up on the back of her neck.

'Are you all right, Max?'

For a second his eyes crinkled, but not in their usual sunny way as his face broke into a smile. Instead, deep, unfamiliar lines grooved the edges of his grey eyes as the beginning of a frown appeared. 'It's nothing,' Max mumbled, fiddling with the salt shaker, which instantly hit her as strange. It was normally Tessa who fiddled, Tessa who played with her food, the sugar bowl, the teaspoons—anything she could get her hands on actually—while Max sat nonchalantly, a look of vague amusement on his carefree face.

'If there's a problem Max, you can talk to me,' Tessa offered tentatively. 'We're friends.'

A look Tessa couldn't quite interpret flashed in his eyes and she was quite sure, as she registered his Adam's apple bob in his throat, that Max was working his way up to tell her something.

'Here you are, Dr Slater, sunny side up, just as you like them.' Like the channels changing on the television, instantly the vision shifted. The wistful moment disappeared and the larrikin was back as Max licked his lips, while Narelle busied herself arranging knives and forks.

Max *always* licked his lips when a plate was put in front of him, Tessa mused. He was the only person who enjoyed food as much as she did. They spent hours, literally hours, talking about recipes and restaurants and the lack of variety in the canteen's machines at night. Mind you, unlike Tessa, Max didn't suffer for his sins. Three bars of chocolate washed down with cola was his usual staple diet on a night shift and not a single globule of fat ended up on his tall wiry frame, whereas Tessa only had to watch him eat to suffer the consequences at the next weigh-in.

'What's this?' Max's fork stopped midway to his mouth as Narelle placed a steaming plate of bacon and eggs in front of Tessa.

'My new diet.' Tessa shrugged. 'It's low carbohydrate, or should I say *no* carbohydrate. Apparently loads of film stars are on it at the moment, the weight's supposed to fall off you. And the best bit of it is that I can eat as much of this as I like.'

'You're not serious?' Max stared incredulously at her heaving plate. 'As much as you like?'

Tessa nodded. 'The more the better. I had this for breakfast as well.'

Max peered at her plate more closely. 'No toast to mop up the yolk?'

'Definitely not.'

'No mushrooms?'

'No.' Tessa shook her head seriously. 'They've got carbohydrates.'

'Fruit?'

Again Tessa shook her head. 'It's this and lots of it—no doubt I'll be having this for dinner later. Apparently I can have cheese as well,' she added with a slightly nauseous twinge to her voice.

'Do you want me to ring Coronary Care now and book you a bed?'

'You can talk,' Tessa snapped indignantly. 'Anyway, at least I'll be thin as they're strapping me to the cardiac monitor.'

'How many times to I have to tell you, Tess? You're fine just as you are.'

'I don't want to be *fine*,' Tessa sighed. 'I want to be thin and gorgeous and slip into tiny little tops and micro-skirts.'

'Yes, please.' Max winked. 'To the skirts and tops I mean. OK, Tess, you're not fine, you're gorgeous and stunningly so—take it from a full-blooded male who knows a thing or three about women. So don't you dare go rotting your health with yet another one of your fad diets.'

Thankfully he chose that moment to dive into his meal, which meant he wasn't a witness to the huge blush that whooshed up Tessa's cheeks as she fumbled with her knife and fork.

'It can't be good for you,' he insisted.

'It's only for a couple of weeks, and for once it has nothing to do with vanity—it's purely a financial thing.' She watched as his forehead creased. 'There was a letter waiting for me from the coroner's court when I got back. I thought the inquest was going to be adjourned but it would seem that it's going ahead at the original date.' Despite the casual smile, Max heard the tremor in her voice. 'And as neither of the two smart suits in my wardrobe will do up any more, it's either this or a major splurge on my credit card.'

'It will be all right, Tess.' Brunch forgotten, Max put down his knife and fork and reached over the table, giving her a friendly pat on the arm. 'You did nothing wrong that night.'

'Let's just hope the coroner agrees.' A moment's silence followed as Tessa wrestled with a sudden surge of tears in her eyes. 'An eighteen-year-old died, Max, in my department, when I was on charge.'

'I hate to state the obvious, Tess,' Max ventured gently. 'But that's par for the course in this line of work.'

'A coroner's investigation isn't the norm, though,' Tessa responded quickly, the anxiety in her voice evident. 'And endless interviews with the hospital's solicitor are hardly part of my job description. If Matthew Benton's death comes down to me I don't think I can bear it.'

'It won't come down to you.' Max's calm voice broke in firmly. 'Hell, Tess, the department was full to bursting and, yes, it was busy, but I've been over and over Matthew's notes and everything that should have been done was done that night. Nothing was amiss, even though the place was busy, he still got all the right treatment.'

'But did he get the best treatment?' Her brown eyes jerked up to meet his, the question she had plagued herself with over and over coming out more forcefully than Tessa had intended. 'I knew how stretched we were, I knew that it was getting dangerously busy. We had ambulances rolling up in pairs, a sick child in Resus, the waiting room bursting at the seams, and then we started to get in the patients from Matthew's car crash.'

'So you did the right thing,' Max reasoned. 'You realised that the place was getting too full, that the staff were being spread too thin, so you did something about it—you put the department on bypass.'

'Ten minutes before the paramedics brought Matthew in. If I'd put the department on bypass earlier, if I'd told Ambulance Control sooner that we couldn't accept any more patients, then they wouldn't have come to us. They'd have taken him to another hospital that wasn't so busy. Maybe there he'd have got better attention...'

'And maybe he'd have died in the ambulance on the way.'

'I know,' Tessa said wearily, massaging her temples with her fingers, closing her eyes against the horrors of that night, but it didn't work. They'd had this conversation numerous times, gone over and over the awful chain of events, but Max showed no impatience at the repetitive nature of the conversation. He, better than anyone, knew how much she needed to talk, needed to go over the jumble of events until hopefully they fell into some sort of order, and he waited patiently as Tessa sat with her eyes closed, struggling to hold it all together. 'I know the outcome would probably have been the same whatever we'd done, I know all that. I'm just dreading it.'

'Look, a day at the coroner's court certainly isn't one of the perks of the job,' Max said with a dry smile, 'but the further you go up the ladder the more it becomes a part of it. We're accountable, Tessa, not just for our own decisions but for the actions of the staff under us, and like it or not, as unfair as it may seem, the buck stops here sometimes.' His hand motioned the two of them and Tessa nodded glumly. 'It isn't a witch hunt, it's about finding the cause of Matthew's death, piecing together the chain of events and seeing if somewhere along the line something could have been done differently. At worst, the hospital might come in for some criticism.' He watched as she flinched. 'And if it does, we'll deal with it,' Max added gently. 'We'll learn from it and make damn sure that any mistakes that were made aren't repeated. You know I'll be there for you.'

'I know,' Tessa mumbled, daring to glimpse at the future when the coroner's court was finally behind her. 'We'll have an extra-long lunch-break and dissect the court case over one of Narelle's muffins.'

'I meant that—I'll come to the coroner's court with you.'

Tessa looked up sharply. 'But you weren't even on duty when it happened.'

'I know, but I figured you could use the moral support, so I've pencilled it in my diary. Dr Burgess will cover the department for me. I quite fancy a day out in the city.'

'I don't think there'll be much time for sightseeing,' Tessa pointed out with a slight edge to her voice.

'I'm playing.' Max smiled. 'I just want to be there for you, I know how worked up you are about this.'

'Y-you're sure,' Tessa stammered, stunned yet thrilled he would do that for her.

'Of course I'm sure—we're friends, aren't we?'

'You know we are.' Tessa nodded gratefully then a teasing half-smile crept across her full mouth. 'Let's just hope it's not adjourned, then.' She watched as Max shuffled uncomfortably in his seat. 'A few—actually, quite a few—little birds have been telling me that my *friend* Max has taken a position in London, an emergency consultant's position, in fact, in a very busy, very respected children's hospital. Of course, I told them they must be mistaken, I mean, surely my *friend* would have told me or at the very least hinted that a move was in the air, not just left me to find out on the hospital grapevine.'

'You've been on a course,' Max mumbled.

'For five days,' Tessa pointed out. 'I hardly think all this was arranged while I was away on a trauma course.'

'I just wanted to keep it under my hat until I knew I had the job.'

'Fair enough,' Tessa relented, but only for a second. 'But you've never even given a hint that you're fed up.'

'I'm not.'

'Then what on earth are you moving to the other side of the world for?'

'Because it's a great job—you know how much I love paediatric emergency.'

'There's a children's hospital in Melbourne,' Tessa retorted, 'with a massive emergency department. If that was what you really wanted to do then I'm quite sure they'd have taken you on.'

'I know,' Max answered uncomfortably. 'It was just too good an offer to turn down.'

'Hmm.' Tess stared across the table, her soft brown eyes still reproachful. 'So some hospital in London urgently needed a doctor and thought, ''Max Slater in Australia would be perfect for the job, let's ring him now.'' Come on, Max, your feelers must have at least been out. You must have applied for it.'

'So?'

'So, when did you start to get itchy feet and why didn't you say anything? I know we're not exactly bosom buddies, but I though we at least went a bit deeper than discussing Narelle's latest creation. I thought you were really happy here.'

'I am.'

'So why are you going?' Hearing a slightly needy note creep into her voice and realising she had probably gone too far, Tessa gave a small shrug and feigned a laugh. 'Sorry, none of my business. I was just looking forward to your wedding—another excuse to go on a diet, if ever I needed one. And I'm peeved because no doubt you'll whisk Emily off to Gretna Green and I'll miss out on a great wedding party and my portion of the wedding cake.'

'Emily's not coming.'

The coffee that was on its way to Tessa's lips stopped midway. Blinking a couple of times, she took a sip, before rather clumsily placing the cup back in its saucer. 'Oh.'

'It's just me that's leaving,' Max added, and his eyes were avoiding Tessa's.

Suddenly Tessa wished that she smoked. Not really, but it would be so nice now to have something to do with her hands, to create a tiny diversion while she flicked open a packet and lit up, a few seconds of grace to collect the rampaging thoughts that were stampeding through her brain.

Another 'Oh' was all Tessa could manage, though, coupled with a slightly dry smile as she imagined Narelle's horror if she had dared to smoke in her beloved canteen.

'We've put the wedding plans on hold.' A smile tugged at the side of his mouth. 'Aren't you going to say ''oh'' again?'

'Oh,' Tessa squeaked, her mind working ten to the dozen.

'Thing's aren't too great between Emily and I at the moment, but that's just between you and me, so don't go firing it around the hospital.'

'I wouldn't,' Tessa said indignantly. 'I only listen to the gossip, I never start it.'

They sat in silence again, but this time it certainly wasn't comfortable. Endless questions bobbed on her tongue, but Tessa bit them back, knowing it was none of her business, knowing Max would tell her only what he wanted to.

'London won't know what's hit them.' It was a small attempt to break the strained atmosphere, a little joke to desperately lighten the mood that had suddenly taken a massive dive. 'You'll have to smarten up a bit.'

'What's wrong with what I'm wearing?' Max replied indignantly, but he was at least smiling now they were on the familiar territory of his appalling dress sense.

'Nothing.' Tessa gave a cheeky wink. 'For a walk along the beach, anyway.'

'They're smart shorts!' Max protested.

'They might be if you ironed them, and I can't really imagine the consultants there wearing T-shirts and boat shoes.' Tessa put up her hands in mock defence as Max opened his mouth to protest. 'Just a mental picture

I've got of London, Max—you know, doctors in smart suits, nurses with starched uniforms and caps.'

'It's the twenty-first century, Tess, that all went out with the ark.'

Tessa laughed. 'I could be wrong, but you're in a little bay-side town here Max, most of the patients know you already, the staff certainly do. We know that under that scruffy hair is a brilliant medical brain.'

'Well, I'm not wearing a suit,' Max shrugged defiantly. 'For anyone.'

Tessa turned back to her coffee staring dreamily out of the window, images of London dancing through her mind—Piccadilly Circus, the Houses of Parliament, tree-lined streets she had seen only in tele-vised weddings and funerals. So far away it might just as well be on another planet, and Max was actually going to be there, riding on the subway or the tube or whatever its name was, having short days and cold Christmases. Her mind danced around London as she sat there. She'd never had any desire to go, it had never even entered her head before. Despite being an eternal romantic, Tessa had her head screwed on firmly enough to realise it wasn't all going to be rosy-cheeked children singing around Christmas trees and rolling English countryside littered with wildlife. And, no doubt, Max would grumble like crazy about the warm beer and the exchange rate, but London…

'Maybe I should get some smart trousers,' Max relented after a few moments' silence, his mind obviously still on the conversation. 'I guess I could buy a couple of shirts as well.'

'A tie even?' Tessa teased, and Max shuddered. 'And while you're at it, you might even get a haircut.'

'You're pushing it now,' Max grumbled. 'Still, I am going to have to start sorting things out, it's only two weeks until I go.'

'Are you excited?'

'Yes and no.' Max shrugged but didn't give any more away.

'It's a big move, though,' Tessa pushed, even though it was obvious that Max wanted to end the conversation. 'You must at least be a bit nervous. Will you miss us all?'

'It's only for a year, Tess,' he said, but the raw note of urgency to his voice had Tessa convinced he was assuring himself more than her. 'Peninsula Hospital will still be here when I get back. I'm just taking a year out—things will stay the same, won't they?' His face was serious, his hand was back on her arm and Tessa swallowed the lump that had mysteriously appeared in her throat. 'You'd do the same, wouldn't you? I mean, if your dream job came up you'd grab it.'

For an age she stared at Max, but it became too hard. Too hard to look him in the eye and tell him she was OK with this. Dragging her eyes away, she drank in the view—the fisherman on the jetty, the endless beach that constantly beckoned her, the jagged rocks full of tiny pools, each one a Pandora's box of treasures she'd gaze into and dream away the hours as she swirled her hands through the water.

Maybe London was glamorous and exciting, but it wasn't home.

'I've got my dream job, Max,' she said softly, her eyes slowly moving back to him. 'OK, it's not the cutting edge of nursing, people aren't going to look at my résumé and shake with excitement, but it's all I want— Charge Nurse of the emergency department at Peninsula. Enough emergencies to keep the adrenaline flowing and plenty of stunning views to calm me down when it all gets too much. This is enough for me, Max. I thought it was for you as well.'

'It is, it's just…' A long-fingered hand ran through his tousled hair and he let out a ragged sigh. 'I need to talk to you, Tess.'

'We are talking,' Tessa said lightly, a forced smile taut on her strained face.

'I mean away from here.' He gestured to the room, his eyes never leaving her. 'Away from the hospital.'

'What about Emily?' Tessa asked slowly.

'She's on call tonight.'

Another wrong answer.

As the shutters came down on her eyes Max broke in quickly. 'I don't mean it like that, Tessa, I just really need to talk to you.'

'No!' Tessa said rather too forcefully. 'It's Emily you should be talking to about any problem you're having with your relationship—she's the one with your ring on her finger. And if it's an impartial, feminine viewpoint you're after, believe me, Max, you're asking the wrong woman.'

'What's that supposed to mean?'

'Well...' Tessa's eyes darted nervously, wishing she could take back the words she had just uttered and frantically searching her mind for a way to diffuse them. 'I'm not exactly an authority on the perfect relationship. Look how many dating disasters I've endured in my time.'

'I'm not asking you out for a counselling session, Tessa, I just want to talk to you.'

'Sorry, Max.' Tessa gave a vague shrug. 'I'm a bit tied up at the moment.'

Never had the chimes of the emergency loudspeaker springing into life been more gratefully received and Tessa jumped up, grabbing her pager from the table as Max reluctantly joined her. 'Come on, it looks like we're wanted.'

'Tessa?' The question in his voice didn't go unnoticed, but so innocent was the smiling face that turned to him, so wide her smile, that Max hesitated, his pensive expression shifting, his own face breaking into a wide smile that matched hers. 'Come on, I'll race you.'

They sped along the corridor, laughing as they did so, Tessa's long brown hair flying behind her as she tried to keep up with Max's effortless strides, their pagers shrilling in their pockets alerting them to head to Emergency as other hospital personnel flattened against the walls to let them past.

And to anyone watching, Tessa didn't look as if she had a care in the world as she burst through the swing doors and headed straight for Resus.

'Beat you.' Max smiled before turning to Jane and getting the run-down of the trauma that was about to come through the doors.

'You always do,' Tessa grumbled as she ran through and set up the necessary equipment.

'Ah, but I had an added incentive to stay ahead of you this morning.' Max grinned as Tessa's forehead creased. 'How many eggs did you say you'd had?'

It was a joke, a below-the-belt joke that nurses and doctors dished out almost by the minute, a brother-sister-type tease that normally Tessa would have shrugged off before it had even registered in her brain.

But it wasn't a normal morning, and there was nothing sisterly about the way Tessa was feeling. Max *was* leaving, there was no denying it now, she'd heard it straight from the horse's mouth.

It really was going to happen.

All that talk, all that bravado about being friends had all been a lie—a lie she was so used to living. After five years it came as naturally as breathing. And her excuse to him about not being able to offer an impartial feminine viewpoint had been another one.

Feminine she could readily manage, but impartial, well, it wasn't even a vague possibility.

Max, with his curly brown hair and teasing smile, had never, since the moment Tessa had first laid eyes on him, been just a friend. Max, with his crumpled clothes and banana-skin humour, who could make her cry with laughter one minute and suddenly be serious the next, was so much more than her work confidant, brunch buddy and sounding-board.

There was nothing impartial about Tessa's feelings.

Max Slater was the man that she loved.

CHAPTER TWO

'SORRY to drag you back, guys. The story's a bit vague from Ambulance Control so I thought it best to be prepared.'

'No problem,' Max replied easily. 'What do we know so far?'

'Speedboat versus jet-ski.'

'Ouch.' Max rolled his eyes. 'How many?'

'Three from the boat, two with seemingly minor injuries and one unconscious, thankfully they were all wearing life jackets.'

'And the jet-skier?' Tessa asked, mentally assessing the injuries and matching her staff available.

'He's not been so lucky, I'm afraid. It would seem he wasn't wearing a life jacket. The report from Ambulance Control is that he's got multiple injuries, including a possible broken neck. They were going to take him straight to the spinal unit, that's why I held off calling you, but apparently he's gone into full cardiac arrest in the helicopter so they're bringing him here.'

The spinal unit was only another thirty minutes or so in the helicopter but, given that full resuscitation was in progress, thirty minutes along the bay was too long and Tessa gave a small grimace. 'Hopefully we can get him there later. How do you want to work this, Jane?'

Technically the allocation was up to Tessa as she was the charge nurse on duty, but Jane was a senior nurse and this morning Tessa had let her be in charge, gradually allowing more responsibility to fall onto Jane's shoulders, with the intention being that she could soon oversee the department by herself.

'Well, I'd like to take the full resus, but I guess if I'm supposed to be running the show I should take the unconscious boat victim and direct traffic.'

'Good call.' Tessa's voice was encouraging, but inwardly she sighed at Jane's persistent lack of foresight. As good an emergency nurse as Jane was, she had rather too much bravado about her and a noticeable unwillingness to delegate, far happier to be in the thick of things than running the show. It was something Tessa was working on quietly, but with rather limited success. 'But the boat victim is an unknown entity. You might find yourself just as tied up with him.'

Jane chewed her lip thoughtfully, and Tessa glanced at her fob watch, willing her colleague to hurry up and make a decision.

'Why don't you send Kim in?' Tessa said finally when it was obviously they weren't getting anywhere.

'But she's only a grad nurse,' Jane protested, itching to pull on her latex gloves and get on with the job she loved.

'A grad nurse who needs more resuscitation experience,' Tessa pointed out. 'First-hand experience is the only way she'll learn and at least Max is on so he'll watch her like a hawk. I can oversee them while I deal with the boat victim.'

'So when I'm in charge I just get to stay in the corridor and direct traffic?'

'Well, there's a bit more than that.' Tessa smiled at her colleague's disappointed face. 'You'll be run off your feet with relatives and us calling for things, but that's the way it is when you're in charge, Jane. Someone has to be the chief.'

'Great,' Jane muttered as Tessa made her way into Resus, more than happy to be in the thick of things again.

'Sorry, guys, I was stuck in Theatre. What's the story?'

Even if Tessa hadn't recognised the voice, the sudden tension that filled the room told Tessa that Emily had arrived and, more annoyingly, Tessa didn't even have to look up to know that the sight that would have greeted her would have been one of unruffled, petite beauty.

Emily never looked ruffled. The woman had probably spent the morning pulling dislocated hips and shoulders into place and yet her blonde hair was pulled back into a perfectly neat ponytail, her theatre blues looked tailor-made and her clear, china blue eyes never wandered as she listened intently to the brief history given by a suddenly nervous Jane.

Emily had that effect on women.

On men, too.

Come to think of it, Tessa grumbled to herself as she assembled equipment, even three-year-olds quaked when Emily approached.

She might look like a tiny fragile porcelain doll, but two minutes in her company soon put paid to that. Emily Elves hadn't made it to orthopaedic registrar courtesy of her good looks, and the fact her father was the top obstetrician in the hospital wouldn't count for anything when she went for the consultant's position at the end of the month. No, Emily had made it this far in a man's world through steely determination, a brilliant medical mind and an utter disregard for emotion.

'So the jet-skier wasn't wearing a life jacket.' Her blue eyes finally swivelled to Max when the history was completed and a wry smile appeared on her smooth face. 'Did you hear that, Max?'

'No doubt it's all I'm going to hear for the next few days,' Max responded with a slight edge to his voice that instantly had the room enthralled.

'You see,' Emily explained, still smiling as she started to pull up some drugs from the trolley, 'Max Slater, your, oh, so responsible emergency consultant, the lynchpin of the department, the one we're supposed to look to for guidance, well, he thought he might try his hand at jet-skiing last weekend.'

Everyone laughed. It was the type of conversation that often took place as the adrenaline kicked in while they waited for the arrival of patients, but even though Tessa joined in the laughter a small frown puckered her brow. As commonplace as this type of conversation might be amongst the staff in Emergency, it was a revelation to hear Emily opening up. Emily Elves was eternally private. In fact, normally she went out of her way to keep her professional and personal lives completely separate, yet here she was for the first time in memory telling anyone who was interested about her weekend with Max. There was definitely something strange going on.

But Tessa had no choice but to listen and laugh along with the rest of the rabble and it hurt.

Really hurt.

'Of course,' Emily continued, 'I knew nothing about it. There I was, having a doze on the beach, half listening as some hoon came in way too close to the shore, laughing his head off, whooping with enjoyment and generally making a nuisance of himself, you get the picture. It was only when the yob in question started calling my name did I sit up and take notice...'

'I was only on the jet-ski for ten minutes,' Max argued. 'If that. Mind you...' he grinned '...it was the best ten minutes of my life.'

'And it could very well have been the last ten minutes,' Emily said pointedly, cocking her head as the sound of the chopper got louder. 'Need I say more?'

Thankfully she didn't. The last thing Tessa needed this morning was cosy little images of Emily and Max at the beach, no doubt with Emily skinny and gorgeous, some tiny little bikini accentuating her smooth brown skin, good-naturedly bickering about Max's casual attitude to the world at large, Max's take-it-or-leave-it slant on things.

It was a relief when the patients arrived and Tessa could concentrate on work.

The first victim to arrive was the unfortunate jet-skier. Though no longer in full arrest, he was still dangerously close to it.

'OK, Kim, just listen to Max, he's supporting the neck so he's the team leader.' Tessa hovered in the background, watching closely as Kim worked intently. As important as it was to give the staff experience, it could never be at the expense of patient care, and in this instance any hesitation could prove fatal. The lift over to the trolley was swift but very controlled, given the likelihood of spinal injuries, and Tessa tried not to interfere too much as she watched Kim's shaking hands change over the equipment from the rescue team's to the unit's own. Already the young man was intubated. The paramedics had put a tube in place in his throat, thus securing the airway, and intravenous access had been established.

'Right, Kim, look at the cardiac monitor. What do you see?'

Kim swallowed hard, her cheeks colouring as she stared at the machine. 'His heart rate's slow.'

'Yep, he's in sinus bradycardia, so what drugs do you think he'll need?'

'Atropine?' The answer was right but Tessa could hear the question in the Kim's voice.

'Good,' Tessa said encouragingly. 'Max is checking his airway now—that's the first priority—but once he looks at the monitor no doubt he'll be calling for atropine or adrenaline so if you can try to preempt what he'll need, you'll have a head start. You may well be wrong but at least it's easier to pull up the drugs and have them ready to hand over to him before he starts calling for them.'

'Atropine.' Max's word was clipped, not even looking up he placed an impatient hand out, and thankfully Kim was able to pass him the drug immediately.

'Get the chest-tube pack out,' Tessa whispered, watching Max frown as he palpated the young man's ribcage and run through a flask of mannitol. As the resus doors slid open and Tessa's patient arrived, she gave her colleague's shoulder a quick squeeze. 'Don't mind Max if he shouts. It's not aimed at you personally, it's just his way.'

It *was* just his way, Tessa thought as she started to work on her own patient, ignoring a rather loud expletive coming from Max's general direction. Max, passionate about every patient, would be working on the young jet-skier as if it were his own family member lying near to death on the resus trolley. And if he lost his temper, if he shouted because the equipment he'd only just asked

for wasn't in his hand *now*, it was easily forgiven. Everyone knew they were watching a
genius at work, and a genius was surely allowed the odd eccentricity.

Unlike Emily, Tessa thought to herself as
she set to work on the latest admission. Not
that Emily wasn't a diligent and talented doctor, but her work technique and bedside manner didn't even begin to compare to Max's.
The young man before them was flailing
around on the gurney, distressed, in pain, terrified and, Tessa thought, confused, which
was more ominous than the rest of his symptoms put together. And with little reassurance
to her patient, Emily commenced her examination as Tessa struggled to hold the young
man down and reassure him.

'Stay still for me.' That was the sum total
of Emily's communication with her patient as
her hands worked their way down his body,
leaving it to Tessa to attempt an explanation.
But explanations were hard to give in the absence of information and Emily, as usual,
was giving nothing away.

Emily worked in a completely different manner to Max. Emotions were kept strictly in check as she thought things through in her own time, and from a nursing perspective she wasn't the easiest doctor to work with. There was no pre-empting her, no little clues along the way, nothing in her calm exterior to indicate what was going in that clever head of hers.

'What's his blood pressure?' Emily's voice was completely calm, as if she were asking if there was any milk in the fridge or if anyone had thought to buy a newspaper this morning. The coffee-room or the resus ward was all dealt with in the same unflappable manner. Her meticulous, very neat little hands methodically examined the restless body.

'It's up,' Tessa said, glancing over at the machine. 'One hundred and ninety on a hundred.'

There was no reaction from Emily as she carried on working her way down the patient. 'Do we have a name?'

'Phil's all we've got at the moment,' a voice called from the back of the room, and Tessa nodded her thanks to the paramedic who was writing up his notes in the corner.

'Phil, try and stay still for me while I examine you.'

Which didn't exactly calm the agitated man down.

'You've been in an accident, Phil,' Tessa added as diplomatically as she could, keeping her voice calm and even as she orientated her patient. 'You're at Peninsula Hospital. Dr Elves here is just going have a look at you.'

'His shoulder's dislocated,' Emily said, more to herself than anyone.

'His oxygen sats are low,' Tessa said grimly, 'even though he's on ten litres of oxygen.'

'Hmm, he's got a few fractured ribs as well.'

Sometimes Tessa wanted to shake Emily. An excellent doctor she might be, but she was a lousy team player. Nothing in her calm expression, her clear blue eyes let the staff know what she was thinking—unlike Max, who wore his heart on the sleeve. Right now Tessa was worried about the head injury. By all accounts, Phil had been unconscious for some time, his agitated ramblings and high blood pressure all indicative of a serious head injury, but Emily, though aware of the facts, seemed more concerned about his shoulder.

'Let's get his shoulder back in place then we'll see where we are.'

'Do you need anything?' Tessa ventured, hoping against hope Emily wasn't going to do the procedure without anaesthetic but knowing the call was Emily's.

'Some traction, please,' Emily said without looking up. 'And make sure the brakes are on the trolley.'

Tessa bit her tongue. Giving the patient pain control now would mask any symptoms of his head injury, but to do it without an-aesthetic would be agony. She watched as Emily slipped off her shoes and realised Phil was going to need all the sweet-talking Tessa could manage.

'It will only take a second,' Emily said assuredly. 'Are you going to provide the traction?'

It was more an order than a request. Reluctantly, and trying hard not to show it, Tessa held onto the unfortunate man's shoulder, watching as Emily placed the ball of her foot in his armpit. For someone so tiny she was incredibly strong, which was an absolute prerequisite in orthopaedics. Leaning back, Emily pulled as Tessa took the head end and utilised every last bit of her strength to hold the trolley steady and provide the necessary traction that would enable Emily to slip the shoulder back into place. Engaged in their own tug of war for a moment, just as Emily had predicted, the shoulder slipped back easily into place and instantly Tessa felt Phil relax under her hands.

Emily was good, Tessa admitted grudgingly.

Very good.

'Better?' Tessa asked gently, smiling as her patient nodded, responding appropriately for the first time since his arrival. His eyes were closed, though, only opening when Tessa spoke.

'It was killing me.'

'Do you know where you are?'

Phil didn't answer immediately, his eyes closing between sentences, and Tessa had to prompt him to stay awake. 'Phil, do you know where you are?'

His battered, sunburnt face turned and stared at the badge hanging around Tessa's neck. 'Hospital?'

Tessa smiled. 'Is that an educated guess?'

'I'm afraid so,' he answered, drifting off again until Tessa none too gently tweaked his ear, which roused him enough for a slightly longer conversation.

'Do you remember anything that hap- pened?' Ticking off Phil's responses in the observation chart, Tessa tried to keep the as- sessment as light as possible. She could see the effort in Phil's face as he attempted to recall the morning's events, see the fear in his eyes, the slight note of panic in his voice, and knew it was only a matter of time before the full impact of what had happened took hold.

'We were just out, doing some waterskiing, having a laugh...' He frowned as loud rhythmic banging came from behind the curtain, and Tessa felt her heart sink as she realised that the other young man had obviously slipped back into cardiac arrest, the rhythmic banging a desperate attempt to massage the stilled heart into action. 'Some kid on a jetski, he'd have only been about nineteen... He just came from nowhere.'

Max's orders were coming thick and fast now, and as she heard his call for two hundred joules Tessa forced her eyes to stay on her patient, listening to the defibrillator charging up behind her. She could hear Jane's voice, so there was no need for her to go and help, but it didn't mean her heart wasn't on the other side of the curtain, willing the young man to pull through.

'Do you remember anything else?' Tessa asked gently, but as Phil went to answer again Max's voice broke in.

'Everybody back.'

Phil lay in agonised silence as the click of the shock being delivered filled the resuscitation room. 'Is that him?'

Technically Tessa didn't need to answer. Discussing other patients was taboo at the best of times but, given that only a thin curtain separated the two patients, it seemed cruel and pointless to dismiss Phil's heavy question with a dismissive shrug, so instead she gave a small nod, watching as Phil's face dropped, placing a gentle hand on his good arm.

'They're doing everything they can.'

'How's it going?' Jane's grim face popped around the curtain.

'Emily's just popped his shoulder back, he's a lot more comfortable.'

'Do you want to move him over to one of the cubicles?' Jane's wide eyes left Tessa in no doubt that the news was only going to get worse for the young jet-skier. And it would probably be kinder to move Phil, less traumatic for him to be in his own space with his own thoughts, rather than listening to the terrible events unfolding a few steps away. Now was a time for one of nursings tough calls. Despite the reduction of his shoulder dislocation, Phil's blood pressure was still dangerously high, and Tessa still wasn't satisfied with his consciousness level. The ease at which he drifted off when she wasn't prompting him worried Tessa, and the thought of him unobserved in a cubicle couldn't be justified because of the traumatic events taking place in the resuscitation room.

'We'll keep him here for now.' Tessa made a small gesture to the monitors and Jane nodded her understanding, moving aside as Luke appeared with the portable X-ray machine and handed Tessa a lead gown.

'I think Max wants a quick C-spine in the next cubicle,' Tessa said in businesslike tones, ignoring the rather eager smile Luke was wearing. Six weeks ago they had shared one very questionable date, and for Luke, at least, it wasn't over yet. 'Then, no doubt, there'll be a pile of films for you to do here.

I'll take a lead gown for the doctors, and Kim next door as well.'

'Tessa.' Kim's call from the next cubicle merited more than a 'yes' and, nodding to Emily, Tessa ducked round the curtain, attempting to slip a very heavy lead coat over Max's head as he examined the patient, tying it up at the sides she tried, and failed, not to notice the musky scent of him, the light hairs on his arms, the quiet strength of his lean body.

He didn't acknowledge her and neither did Tessa expect him to.

'Sorry to be a pain,' Kim started, as Tessa offered to slip a protective coat gown on her, her face red from the exertion of giving cardiac massage. 'It's just...I'd rather not be here while they do the X-rays.'

Her already red face was almost beetroot now and Tessa felt sorry for her. That was the trouble with nursing: nothing was sacred. The fact Kim didn't want to stay while the films were being done could only mean she was either pregnant or hoping to be, and while most of the general population were able to sit on their secrets, emergency nurses didn't have that luxury. Though Tessa's curiosity was naturally aroused, she didn't show it.

'Sure,' Tessa said lightly. 'You take over Phil next door and duck outside while the X-rays are being done.'

'I'm sorry,' Kim said again, needlessly. 'I should have said something earlier.'

'That's the trouble with this place,' Max said dryly, 'it's never early enough. Go,' he said with a small wink. 'Tessa and I know now, that's enough to be going on with, and don't worry about Fred here.' He gestured to the anaesthetist who looked up at the mention of his name. 'We'll cover for you till you're ready for the world at large. Isn't that right, Fred?'

'Sure,' Fred mumbled, obviously bemused at what he was agreeing to.

'Thanks, guys.'

Taking over the massage, Tessa called Kim back. 'Phil's upset about this one,' she said in low tones, 'but I don't think he's well enough to be moved. I know that he looks pretty good on paper, but I'm not happy with him.'

'What does Emily say about him?' Max asked, not even bothering to look up from the array of monitors he was watching like a hawk.

'Not much,' Tessa said tactfully. 'She's reduced his shoulder, so he's a lot more settled. She'll probably do another neurological assessment now that he's calmer.'

'Well, keep a close eye on his neuro obs, and if you're worried, I'm only here,' he offered, which was the closest to an acknowledgment of Emily's poor communication skills they were going to get.

'Sure.'

Fred spoke with an air of weary resignation. 'Max, we've been going for fifteen minutes with no response—there's been nothing since he arrested in the ambulance.'

'He had a pulse when they pulled him out of the water, and a pulse when he first arrived here,' Max snapped, but the anaesthetist shook his head.

'Yes, but he wasn't breathing, heaven only knows for how long. His neck's broken, he's got multiple injuries—'

'Let's just wait for the X-ray, shall we.' It wasn't a question, it was a statement, and Fred shrugged and raised his eyebrows at Tessa who, in an attempt at diplomacy, said nothing. There was nothing unkind in Fred's words or actions, just the awful deliverance of the truth.

But Max didn't want to hear it.

Fred held the X-ray film against the patient's neck as Luke lined up the machine for his shot.

'What time do you finish, Tessa? I thought we might hit that new wine bar that's opened.' Luke's apparent casualness belied his slightly nervous stance.

'I don't think so,' Tessa said abruptly, annoyed with Luke not only for embarrassing her but also for his blatant disregard for the patient. Unconscious he might be, but attempting to arrange a date when a young man lay desperately ill was pushing the boundaries of decency in Tessa's book.

Max's, too, from the dark look he shot at them both.

'I'll take over the massage.' Max moved in, clearly annoyed. 'You wait outside.'

Tessa shook her head. 'I'm fine,' she said quickly. 'We've already had one change-over with the massage, it's better not to disrupt things again. Anyway, it's only one X-ray and I've got a protective gown on.'

'Which isn't done up,' Max pointed out. 'Hold on a second, Luke.'

Like a reflex action, Tessa pulled in her stomach as Max came around, his deft hands pulling the ties together as Tessa worked seemingly unruffled by his closeness. 'Got to protect those ovaries.'

Another tiny comment, another little reference to her femininity, and from anyone else it would have left her mind as soon as it had been said.

But that was the problem with being in love.

Every tiny statement, every throw-away comment was stored and filed then taken out later, poured over and analysed. And every touch, however fleeting, however unambiguous, registered like a size five earthquake on the Richter scale.

It took every ounce of Tessa's professionalism to carry on counting in her mind as she carried on the massage.

The X-rays seemed to take for ever to be developed. Tessa carried on with the massage as Max snapped his orders to a flustered Kim, who was running between the two beds. He used every drug on the trolley and a few more, gave the young man every last shot, used every trick in the book in an attempt to get his youthful heart started, but when Luke came back and pushed the film on the viewfinder Tessa knew at a glance it had all been futile.

For a moment or three Max stared, taking the film down and holding it up to the light as if a different view might make the terrible image look different.

'Max.' It was all she said but it was enough to break the awful loaded silence.

'Maybe we should try...' he began, his eyes darting to the drug trolley, his hands reaching for the internal telephone.

Max could summon who he liked to the department, use every last drug on the trolley, surf the net for any breakthroughs since yesterday with spinal injuries, but for the young man who lay on the resuscitation no amount of technology was going to save him, and the horror of his X-ray only confirmed the fact.

He was beyond saving.

'Max.' Tessa said again this time more definitely as Fred swivelled his eyes between them.

Max nodded then, the tiniest briefest of nods as he replaced the receiver in its cradle. 'Stop the massage.'

Only then did Tessa stop. It had been Max's call and she knew how hard it had been for him to make it. The three stood there, waited and watched the machines, because that was what they had to do, that was what protocol dictated.

It was Fred who moved first, flicking off the monitor and turning off the oxygen when the miracle they had all been secretly hoping for didn't materialise. 'Sorry, guys.'

Nobody spoke as Max performed his final examination. 'Time of death, twelve fifty-two.' He didn't write it down, just stood for a quiet moment, his fists clenched in a strange, defiant sort of salute, then strode off, as Tessa wrote the time in her notebook, knowing Max would need it later.

'Sorry,' Fred said again. 'It's horrible, losing them when they're this young.' Shaking his head, he gave Tessa a weary smile. 'I wouldn't like to be around Max in London, when it's little children lying on the resus bed. It's going to hurt like hell there.'

The fact Tessa didn't know her patient's name didn't stop her from caring, didn't stop the sting of tears in her eyes when she looked at the young body before her. Yes, it was part of the job and, yes, she was used to dealing with death, but the professionalism ingrained into her, the familiar scenario of an emergency room, didn't provide enough of a buffer for the emotions that assailed her. Fred was right, the loss of a young life hurt like hell.

Always would.

Somewhere she had read or heard that a spirit stayed with the body for a while, and though Tessa really didn't know if that was true or not, the thought made her stay a while longer than needed. A moment or two of gentle talk and a little prayer because maybe, and again she wasn't sure, maybe it helped. And when there was nothing more she could do, she quietly made her way out from the curtain.

'No good, huh?'

Phil was still staring at the ceiling, a salty tear slipping down his temple into his hair.

'No,' Tessa said softly. 'I'm sorry you had to hear all that.'

'Don't worry about me, love. In some ways it was better.' He gave a very wobbly smile. 'Better than being just told he died, that I'd just killed someone.'

'It was an accident, Phil,' Tessa pointed out, but he just shook his head, refusing her crumbs of comfort.

'I got up this morning and the sun was shining and all I could think was what a great day it was to be alive. You just never know how your life's going to change, do you? Still, at least I know you all did your best for him, I know that he was given every chance. I'm just going to have to learn how to live with it now.'

'Go and grab a coffee,' Kim mouthed over the patient, and even though Tessa didn't particularly want a drink, even though she knew that Kim was just as upset as she was, Tessa also knew that in a few moments she'd have to face the relatives.

Five minutes out was too good to pass up.

'Before you say "I can't save them all," I know all that.' Max was staring out of the window, his shoulders hunched as if there was a cold wind, not even bothering to turn as Tessa tentatively came into the staffroom.

For a second she wondered how he had known it was her, but she didn't say anything, just stood at the door, watching Max, feeling his pain and wishing more than anything in the world that she could go over and put her arms around him, somehow ease some of the agony she knew that he was feeling.

But it wasn't her place.

'Here…' Walking over, she handed him the casualty card which Max stared at for a moment. 'You'd best write it up while it's still fresh in your mind.'

'As if I'm going to forget.' Tossing the card down, he moved nearer the window. 'Did you finish arranging your date with Luke?'

There was a spiteful note to his voice that Tessa for the moment ignored, choosing instead to put him right in a calm and matter-of-fact voice. 'It was Luke who was inappropriate in there, Max, not me.'

Tessa's apparent calmness only accentuated his pettiness and Max at least had the grace to look shamefaced. 'I'm sorry.'

'What's going on, Max?' She watched as he stiffened, and though her question was bold and direct, there was nothing brave about how Tessa was feeling. She had only been gone a week, but in that short space of time so much seemed to have changed. Something had happened, not just between Max and Emily, not just the fact he was leaving for London. Their friendship seemed to have shifted, subtly perhaps but there was a definite move away from the easy comradeship they had enjoyed for the last five years, a definite shift in Max's demeanour towards her.

'Nothing's going on,' Max finally answered. 'I just didn't like the way Luke was behaving. I shouldn't have taken it out on you, I know you've got more integrity than to speak over a patient like that.'

She could have pushed, could have insisted on a deeper response, but even as Tessa opened her mouth to probe further, she knew she wasn't going to. Max wanted to talk, he'd already told her that, and though a cosy meal might answer a few of her questions, it could only generate a multitude of others.

It was far easier to accept his explanation, to shrug it off with an easy smile and return the conversation to the more familiar territory of Tessa's dating disasters.

'Anyway, for your information, there's not going to be another date. One was more than enough. Luke bored me senseless.'

'He seems nice.' Max shrugged.

'You didn't have to go out with him,' Tessa said, rolling her eyes. 'All he talked about was work.'

'All *we* talk about is work,' Max pointed out.

'Well, at least it's interesting. I now know how many gamma rays it takes to get a decent view of a gallbladder, how long it takes for a barium swallow to work its way through the digestive system.' They were finally smiling at each other, chatting away as they always did, analysing Tessa's appalling love life, just as they'd done for years...

So why did it feel so strained?

'I'd better do these notes.' Picking up the casualty card, Max rummaged in his pocket. 'Have you got a pen?'

Tessa handed him one. 'That's the second one I've given you today,' she pointed out. 'I'm going to buy you one on a rope to wear around your neck.' Her very poor attempt to lighten the atmosphere went without comment and for an age nothing was said, with Tessa doing nothing to break the silence as Max wrote the notes on the back of the card.

'I didn't get the time of death.' Max's pen paused over the page and she watched as he swallowed hard.

'Twelve fifty-two,' Tessa said softly, watching as the pen jerked across the page, feeling the agony behind each word that he wrote. 'Max, don't bite my head off again, but you do know that you did everything possible in there to save him, don't you?'

'I know that.' The bitter edge to his voice had gone, replaced instead by weary resignation. 'In fact, I knew it was over as soon as he hit the department, I knew he was finished before we'd even started.'

'It would have been nice to have been proved wrong for once.' Pushing aside a pile of well-thumbed magazine, Tessa perched on the coffee-table. Picking up the remote, she flicked off the television blaring in the corner.

Silence seemed somehow more fitting.

'He was nineteen, Tessa. Nineteen years old, fit and strong with everything ahead of him, and there wasn't a single thing I could do to save him.'

'Not a single thing,' Tessa said very deliberately. 'But sometimes you *are* proved wrong Max, we all are. Every now and then a patient comes in that we're all sure won't make it and despite all the odds, despite the worse predictions, it all comes together, whether it's medicine or a miracle. Every now and then we're glad to be proved wrong, and that's why we do it. That's why we give the patients the benefit of the doubt and go on working on them long after logic says stop, long after the textbooks say it's over, because occasionally miracles do happen.'

'Just not today.' Grey eyes turned to her and she ached, physically ached to go over to him. 'As soon as Luke put the X-ray up, I knew there was nothing we could do.'

'Are you sure you're doing the right thing? This new job I mean?' It was a candid question, but it wasn't a loaded one. Despite Tessa's internal objection to Max going, she truly didn't have a secret agenda here, just a genuine concern for her colleague and friend. 'Won't this new job be too much for you?'

He almost smiled. 'Are you psychic or something? I've been standing here wondering the same thing.' He ran a weary hand across his forehead. 'You'd think that I'd be used to it by now. Maybe I shouldn't let it get to me so much.'

'I think you're a better doctor because it *does* get to you,' Tessa volunteered, blushing to her roots as she did so. 'I know if it was me or mine on that resus bed I'd want a doctor who cared, one who was prepared to give me the benefit of the doubt. But we're not talking about the patients here, Max, we're talking about the effect it has on you. I've worked with you for five years, we've had this conversation more times than I can count, but at least they're relatively few and far between and nine times out of ten it's someone elderly. I know it still hurts, I know it's still sad, but at least you can console yourself that they've had a life. What's it going to be like in a children's hospital? When every death is agony?'

'It's not all about death.'

'I know, Max. I know there'll be more wins than losses, more saves than misses, we both know the platitudes, we've said them until we're blue in the face, but you take a piece of each one with you, it hurts you more perhaps than most. How are you going to be on the other side of the world when all the losses, all the misses are children?'

'You mean, who's going to come into the coffee-room and give me a pep talk?'

He was smiling now, his eyes crinkling in that endearing way, and the blush that had just about faded from Tessa's face returned with venom. 'Oh, I'm sure the staff will be just as nice. No doubt, there'll be nurses falling over themselves to console you.'

'It won't be the same, though.' His face was suddenly serious. 'It's starting to all sink in now I've actually handed in my notice and it's all official. It's starting to hit me that I'm really going.'

You don't have to, Tessa wanted to say, but knew it wasn't what he needed to hear. Instead, she tucked her hands under her legs, a rather pathetic safeguard to keep her hands where they should be, so tempting was it to reach out to him.

'I can't imagine getting up each day, going to work, drinking my coffee, moaning about the traffic or the weather.' He smiled, but it was loaded with sadness. 'I just can't imagine doing all that each day...' His voice trailed off and Tessa stared at the floor, waiting to hear about the comradeship in the department, the friends he'd made, the team he'd built—braced herself even for an endearing reference to Emily. But what Max said, the words that filled the still silent coffee-room made Tessa eternally grateful that she had sat down when she'd entered. Only her eyes jerked up as he spoke, confusion flickering there, her mouth literally dropping open as his eyes searched her face for a reaction.

'I just can't picture myself, Tessa, can't quite picture doing all of this without seeing you.'

CHAPTER THREE

'CAN I have a word, Tessa?'

How Tessa would have loved to have said no to Kim's request, to have shaken her head and kicked the door shut, to turn to Max and ask just what he'd meant by that, just what the hell had got into him this morning. But, of course, she didn't. Swallowing hard, she tore her eyes away from Max, registering he looked as stunned by his words as Tessa had felt on hearing them.

'Sure, Kim.'

'I'll leave you to it.' Max's voice for once sounded anything but confident and Tessa was positive there was a hint of a blush darkening his face.

'It's OK, Max, you don't have to go,' Kim offered. 'I'm sure you've worked out what it's about.'

'Uh-oh.' Max put his hands up to his ears and shook his head. 'Sounds like secret women's business. I'm out of here.'

Kim laughed. Even Tessa managed a half-hearted attempt at a smile but her mind was still working overtime, was still reeling from what Max had said, to give an Oscar-winning performance. He stopped at the door, turned and gave that endearing smile.

'Am I allowed to say congratulations?'

'Not yet.' Kim held up her crossed fingers. 'I'll be twelve weeks on Friday, touch wood. You can save it for then.'

'Do you want to go through to the office?' Tessa suggested, and Kim nodded gratefully. Typical emergency nurses, they made a quick coffee before heading off, careful not to miss an opportunity for a caffeine hit.

'How's Phil doing?' Tessa asked when she realised Kim wasn't quite ready to open up.

'He's gone for a CAT scan. Emily went with him, she's finally admitted that she's worried about his head injury. She's so hard to work with,' Kim moaned. 'Give me Max any day.'

'I know Emily can seem difficult,' Tessa said quickly, keen to dispel any bad feelings before they blew up—complaints about Emily's bedside manner were becoming rather too familiar. 'But she's a brilliant doctor.'

'Oh, I'm sure she is,' Kim said, though she sounded far from convinced. 'But take it from a grad nurse, sometimes the odd word of encouragement wouldn't go amiss. The only reason she doesn't have me in floods of tears like the rest of the grads and junior staff is because I'm in my thirties. I've got enough life experience not to let her aloofness get to me.'

'It's just the way she works. Look, Kim, orthopaedics is very male-dominated. Emily's only too aware, in the nicest way possible, that she's very blonde, very small and very pretty. Imagine how hard it must be for her. Every time she stops for a chat or a giggle she's seen as shallow, every time she gets upset about a patient they blame it on hormones.'

'Well, I can sympathise with that,' Kim sniffed.

'Just bear it in mind. Everything Emily does she has to do ten times better to get any credit. It's no wonder she's focussed. Just don't take it personally.'

'OK.' Kim nodded. 'I'll try. Hey, did you see her necklace, loads of tiny little shells?'

'Don't tell me.' Tessa rolled her eyes and took off her charge nurse hat for a moment, not wanting to come across as impervious to Kim's very real concerns. 'Emily made it herself. Is there anything that woman can't do?'

They shared a little laugh and the tension was broken. A naturally nosy person, Tessa was curious but not in a malicious way. She loved the opportunity nursing gave her to glimpse into people's lives, and as a manager she was now afforded the same insight into her colleagues, her status delivering the unspoken word that the conversation wouldn't leave the room.

'Am *I* allowed to say congratulations?' Tessa ventured, slightly startled by the tears that suddenly appeared in Kim's eyes.

'Yes, please.'

Wrapping her friend and colleague in a hug, Tessa pulled a box of tissues from the desk.

'I'm sorry I didn't say anything,' Kim started. 'I didn't think I'd need to just yet, I don't usually end up in Resus.'

'Hey, you don't have to say anything now,' Tessa insisted. 'There's a good reason you don't want to be exposed to X-rays, that's all I need to know. You only have to tell me more if you want to.'

'I do want to,' Kim said fiercely. 'I've been holding it in for weeks now. I think I'll burst if I don't talk to someone about it.'

'Does Mark know?' Tessa ventured, relieved when Kim nodded and managed a shaky laugh.

'It's all we talk about.' Blowing her nose loudly, she took a deep breath. 'We've been married for fifteen years. The first ten were spent trying to have a baby,' Kim whispered. 'It nearly tore us apart. So many let-downs, nights crying, doctor's appointments, ultrasounds, blood tests, hormone injections, IVF, GIFT—I've been there and done all that more times than I can count.'

'Got the T-shirt to prove it,' Tessa said dryly, and Kim nodded.

'Every where I looked, friends, family, even strangers in the street, well, they all seemed to either be pregnant or pushing a pram, and the resentment just built up and up. Even something as basic as going to the supermarket was a nightmare in itself. You've no idea how appealing those rows of nappies and baby wipes look when you're on the treadmill of trying to get pregnant.'

'It sounds like hell,' Tessa said gently.

'It was. And then one day I woke up to myself, realised I'd nearly lost my husband, that I'd lost ten years of my life in the eternal quest to have a baby.' She looked up at Tessa. 'I'm not exaggerating. It was all I thought about, all I wanted, and it wasn't getting me anywhere. So I did something about it—booked Mark and I on a dream holiday that we couldn't possibly contemplate with a baby, bought a wardrobe of new clothes, made a list...'

'I make lists.' Tessa grinned. 'Do you divide up the paper?'

'Yep. On one side I had ''Baby,'' on the other was ''Mark, holidays, money, a career I love.'' That's why I'm the oldest grad nurse in town. I'd put so much into trying to get pregnant I'd let the rest of my life slide.'

'But look at you now,' Tessa enthused. 'You're a fabulous emergency nurse.'

'Honestly?'

'Honestly,' Tessa said. 'I wouldn't say it otherwise.'

'I'd actually got used to the idea of not having a baby, finally realised there was more to life than that little pink bundle. Then a few months ago Mark raised it again, said how technology had come on, that maybe it was worth one more try. And even though we're really happy now, even though a baby's not the be-all and end-all, I jumped at the chance. Can you see now why I don't want the news getting out? I couldn't bear all the sympathetic stares if it doesn't work out and I don't want Heather, the unit manager, thinking I've got my head in the clouds chasing baby dreams when she comes to choosing which grad to employ. If I lose the baby I know I'm going to be devastated and I'll need my job more than ever to keep my feet on the ground.'

Tessa listened carefully, yet again floored at the complicated lives people led, the tears behind the smiles that she knew only too well, but at least in this case there was some comfort she could offer and she was only too happy to put Kim's mind at rest. 'I know I shouldn't be telling you this, and I'm trusting you to keep this under your hat for now, but I did your report with Heather last week and we're going to offer you a permanent position in the department once your grad year's over.'

'Were,' Kim said resignedly.

'Are,' Tessa said emphatically. 'You're not the first nurse to get pregnant, and I don't mean that in a glib way—I feel like a pregnancy counsellor some days! And most nurses have a crisis of confidence wondering how they're going to juggle children and a career. It would seem that it's one of life's eternal conundrums, and par for the course in a predominantly female profession, so don't even think about worrying about your job.'

'Thanks, Tessa,' Kim said tearfully. 'Believe me, it's a problem I'd love to have, but I daren't let myself worry about it, at least, not yet anyway—it's the pregnancy I'm concentrating on for now. If I can just get through till Friday I might actually start to believe it's going to happen. I can't wait to be in here bending your ears about maternity leave and days off in lieu.'

'Roll on Friday.' Tessa smiled before glancing down at her watch. 'We'd best get back out there.'

*   *   *

'We've got a name.' Max's tone was businesslike as Tessa walked up to the whiteboard. 'Ricky Hunt. Turns out he's not nineteen, tomorrow would have been his eighteenth birthday. His parents have just arrived.'

'Do they know?'

Max shook his head. 'And there was me thinking it was rough in there.' He gestured to Resus with an air of resigned weariness. 'Here comes the really hard part.'

Of course, because Tessa really needed to talk to Max, really need a postscript to the little bomb he'd dropped, not one opportunity presented itself. Once Max had delivered the awful news, most of Tessa's shift was taken up comforting Ricky's parents, trying to somehow make this bleak dark day no worse for them by an insensitive word, trying not to let the routine of the hospital invade on this awful private time. And finally, when she surfaced, when the roster caught up with her and there was a pile of voicemail messages awaiting her response, whatever mood had taken Max in the coffee-room had long since departed. He smiled his usual smile, gave his usual requests, imparted his corny jokes and basically carried on as if nothing had happened.

Perhaps nothing had happened, Tessa decided, letting herself into her house and slipping off her shoes with an exaggerated sigh. If Kim hadn't come in when she had, maybe Max would have added a multitude of names to the one he'd mentioned.

But...

She tried so hard not to go there. Tried so hard not to dwell on his words, not to let her imagination wander, but Tessa knew it was an impossible feat. Grabbing her wrap, she headed to the beach, hoping that the setting sun and the emerging stars would work their usual magic, help put her jumbled world into perspective.

There was a strange comfort in her insignificance as she walked through frothing surf, feeling the pull of the waves against her ankles, the invigorating whip of the wind on her cheeks. Laying down her wrap, Tessa sank to the sandy carpet and took up her regular ringside seat, looking up at the now darkened sky, watching the flickering lights of a silver plane lifting through the dusky night, dividing and uniting with its cold silver tail.

She had awoken this morning with a naïvety she now yearned for, totally oblivious to the news that was coming, the piece of gossip that would be passed to her like a baton in a relay, and it was up to Tessa to run with it, to arrange the farewell party, to wave the inevitable brown envelope under people's noses and shop for a supposedly suitable gift. Funny, she'd actually braced herself for it, but the brown envelope that Tessa had envisaged had been for a wedding gift for the happy couple, not a leaving present for Max.

Pushing her toes into the sand, Tessa bit hard on her lips then finally gave in to the turbulent emotions that she had kept in check all day, allowing the salty tears to slide down her cheeks, the choked gasps to escape from her throat as she contemplated the turn of events, the awful role of the dice that simultaneously bought her time yet gave her nothing. Trying to decide which of the two evils was worse: losing every last glimmer of hope when Max and Emily finally named the day...

Or losing Max for ever.

CHAPTER FOUR

'MAY I say you're looking particularly fetching this morning, Tessa?'

Max's dry comment didn't faze Tessa for a moment. Dressed in a large green theatre gown, her legs encased in gumboots with a sling wrapped around her dark curls, she knew she looked a sight. The humour in her voice came from the delicious knowledge that she was about to have the last word.

'Thanks, Max.' He was sitting with Fred, both men were eating large ice creams, devouring them actually, which looked a bit strange given that the nine a.m. news was only just coming on the television, but, then, according to the night staff Max and Fred had been there since three that morning. 'It was you that examined Josie Mitchell, wasn't it?'

'Yep.' Max said without looking up, his eyes back on the television. 'She just needs

her varicose ulcer re-dressed. They're looking a bit infected and her chest sounds a bit
rattly, so I've given her an IM injection of
penicillin and a bottle of antibiotics from the
ward stock. There's no way she'd go and get
a scrip dispensed.'

He was right. Josie was one of their regular
homeless people and whatever care could be
squeezed into her sporadic visits generally
was.

'You haven't written up her card yet.'

'I didn't have a pen.'

'Well, when you finally get around to it,
there's a little postscript you might want to
add to your findings.' Tessa paused for effect.
'You'll be pleased to know she's alive.'
Tessa smiled, watching as Max popped the
last of his cone into his mouth.

'Glad to hear it,' he said, completely missing the point.

'I'm not talking about a pulse here, Max.
Your patient is crawling, literally crawling—
at least, her clothes and hair are.'

'Oh, no,' Max groaned.

'Oh, yes.' Tessa grinned. 'Kim and I are just about to delouse her. I thought I'd bring you round a little present before you take your morning shower.' With some relish she handed him a couple of tubes. 'Leave it in your hair for ten minutes and remember all your little creases,' Tessa said with a wicked wink, as Fred not too subtly moved from the seat beside Max and crossed the room.

'Great,' Max grumbled, immediately starting to scratch. 'Just great.'

Tessa laughed. 'One of the perks of the job, I'm afraid. Don't you just love Emergency?'

Bathing Josie was rather like trying to get a very angry, very slippery cat into the water. Getting Josie to agree to the bath was no problem, so long as they promised not to get her beloved Walkman wet, and applying the cream and shampoo no trouble, but, as was so much Josie, the second they lowered the large hoist into the warm soapy water she struggled, kicked and screamed as if they were killing her.

'Nearly there, Josie,' Tessa said firmly above the screams, pushing the 'down' button with one hand as she held onto her patient's wrists with the other, as an already drenched Kim tried to keep Josie's legs from flailing over the side. But the second Josie was in, as soon as the warm soapy water lapped over her body, she relaxed.

'Ooh, lovely.'

'Why do you always fight us, Josie?' Tessa asked. 'You love your bath when you're in it.'

'I do, don't I?' Josie said, as if it were a revelation. 'You can leave me now.'

'I'm supposed to stay,' Tessa pointed out.

'Why? I'm in my seventies, for heaven's sake. Can't I have a bit of privacy at this time of my life?'

'Fair enough,' Tessa agreed. 'I'll go to the cupboard and see about getting you some fresh clothes, but no trying to get out.' Tying the call bell to the handrail at the side of the bath, she showed Josie how it worked. 'I mean it, Josie, no trying to get out by yourself. If you slip, you'll end up on the orthopaedic ward for the next six weeks,' she warned, knowing Josie's hatred of hospitals.

'Am I too late for breakfast?' Josie asked hopefully as the bubbles popped around her, the water already turning a dark muddy brown.

'Way too late,' Tessa remonstrated, then smiled at her most difficult patient. 'But I'll see if I can arrange an early lunch.'

'Stay outside the door,' Tessa warned Kim as they stepped outside. ' I don't care if the emergency bells go off in Resus, you stay here, and if you hear so much as an untoward splash, then stick your head in—Josie will be trying to get out. Don't trust her for a minute.'

'You've got a soft spot for her, haven't you?' Kim grinned.

'She's adorable,' Tessa conceded. 'The old dragon. Did you know she's a bit of a celebrity? Do you ever listen to talk-back radio?'

Kim nodded, obviously bemused. 'Sometimes.'

'You see that Walkman she's always got on? It's permanently tuned into the talk-back radio station. Her only expenditure is batteries and money for the payphone. Every now and then she rings up the station and because she's so articulate and well spoken they give her heaps of air time. It's hilarious, you should listen out for her.'

'The things you learn in Emergency,' Kim said with a grin as Tessa wandered off to the store cupboard.

'How's Josie?' Max had followed her into the cupboard, rubbing his hair with a hospital towel, the white tie on his theatre blues slung low on his waist. She could feel his eyes on her as she stepped up onto a footstool and rummaged through the shelves. Most of the clothes that filled the cupboard were from donations, but every now and then Heather the Nurse Unit Manager took herself off to the Op Shop when supplies were getting low. It was nice to be able to offer the homeless patients the chance of a clean set of clothes occasionally and, given their nature, it was a treat that was never abused.

'In the bath, soaking away,' Tessa answered abstractedly, rummaging through the racks.

'I could hear her screaming from the changing rooms.'

'She hates getting wet. So do I,' Tessa added, flicking her damp fringe out of her eyes. 'Anyway, she's flea-free now. Did you leave the shampoo on for ten minutes like I said?'

'Yes, Sister,' Max answered dutifully. 'I hate the smell of that stuff.'

'It grows on you.' Pulling out a large green coat, Tessa fluffed it out then shook her head as she put it back on the shelf.

'What's wrong with that one?'

'It's green. I tried to give it to Josie last time she came in but she refused and insisted on keeping that shabby old coat of hers. ''Red and green should never be seen,'' she quoted in that snobby, patronising voice of hers. Don't you just love her? She still thinks she's got a head of red curls. I can't bear to tell her she's totally grey. It's a shame because it's a nice warm coat, this one.' She was rambling now, terribly, but Max alone with her in this confined space was giving her the most awful verbal diarrhoea.

'Has she ever told you what happened?' Max's voice was serious. He was leaning against the cupboard door, settling in for a chat and obviously in no hurry to leave, and was doing terrible things to Tessa's blood pressure. 'I mean, has she ever told you how she ended up on the streets? From the way she talks, she's obviously well educated, she must have come from a good family.'

'Who knows?' Tessa said thoughtfully, her mind thankfully slipping away from Max as she pondered one of her favourite patients. 'Just because her parents were affluent it doesn't mean they were good parents. I think Josie had a baby at some point, or there was a child.'

'Did she tell you?' Max perked up, the way you did when a jigsaw was about to be completed, but Tessa shook her head, instantly dispelling an easy solution, and Max leant heavily back against the door as she carried on talking.

'Not directly. She came in one night rambling about babies and punishments and the like, but she's never mentioned it again. I've tried talking to her but she just closes up. She obviously doesn't want to go there.'

'Maybe it's for the best.'

'Do you think so?' The interest in Tessa's voice was genuine. Emergency was a strange place. The patients spent only a relatively short time in one's care but their impact was huge. Sometimes it was nice to take five, to delve a little deeper into their lives. And anyway, she loved Max's insights—his view on the world always slightly different from the norm. 'I thought psychiatry was all about opening up, dealing with the past, coming to terms with things.'

'I'm not a psychiatrist,' Max pointed out. 'And with good reason. I just think some things are best left, some memories are maybe too painful to revisit.'

'Perhaps,' Tessa agreed. Catching his eye, Max was suddenly flying back into her consciousness at an alarming rate, their close proximity registering again. He smiled then, nothing extraordinary in that, Max smiled often, but this one was just for her. For an age he stared as Tessa's colour deepened, and when the silence had gone on for far too long he gave a little embarrassed cough. Flicking up his hand, he pulled down a jumble of shawls and scarves.

'Give her this as well.' Max tossed a blue scarf across the cupboard. 'Tell her, ''Red and green should never be seen unless there's a colour in between''—that's the full saying.'

'Good idea. What *will* we do without you?' It was a light-hearted comment that belied her heavy heart, and stretching to sort out the chaos she'd created on the shelves Tessa automatically pulled her top down over her bottom, painfully aware it wasn't exactly trim, taut and terrific.

That tiny gesture bought an unseen smile to Max's lips, made his throat constrict so hard for a second there he had to struggle to even out his breathing. Tess was so sweet, so utterly and completely adorable, her insecurities so completely unmerited, he had to physically resist the urge to tell her so...

To tell her she was beautiful and kind and good, that there was nothing, nothing she needed to hide from him, nor would there ever be.

But did Tessa want to hear it?

Stepping down off the footstool, he caught her arm to help her, the feel of her skin soft and warm beneath his fingers broiling his senses, her damp fringe hanging over one questioning eye. His grip on her arm tightened as he struggled not to smooth her hair out of her face, to take her soft cheeks in his hands and kiss that delicious full mouth. And though he knew this wasn't the time or the place, though the mental coin he tossed told him to leave things well alone for now, an eternal optimist, he tossed again, moving on to the best out of three, the best out of five, but the answer to his question was still unforthcoming.

She loves me; she loves me not.

'What are you looking so serious about?' With her usual bright smile Tessa looked up at him, her own hand flicking away her fringe, that single gesture ramming home the void that stood between them.

'I was just wondering if you'd miss me.'

'Of course we'll miss you.' Tessa gave a nervous giggle, the small storeroom as stifling as a sauna as she fought to keep her cool.

'I meant, will *you* miss me?'

Max's arm was still there. Suddenly the cupboard was suffocatingly small, she almost heard the hiss as a ladle of water was poured over the hot coals and the temperature went up a notch. His eyes were boring into her, and she truly couldn't read the expression in them, sure on the one hand that the joking

was over but terrified she might be misinterpreting things and utterly confused at the
change in Max's demeanour.

Oh, Max.

His hair was drying now, the brown curls
springing into their usual chaotic shape, and
she physically ached to put up her hand to
run it through the damp newly washed ten-
drils, to run her fingers along his clean-
shaven jaw and to press her lips to his.

How she'd miss him. Words didn't even
come close.

'You know I will...' Her eyes worked the
small cupboard, desperate for a distraction,
but the scent of him filled her nostrils, that
masculine undertone so familiar. Hell, this
man even managed to make gamma benzene
hexachloride smell vaguely sexy. Tessa was
assailed with a vision of volunteering to delouse all the waifs and strays for the next year
in a strange quest to somehow relive this moment. Relive the feel of standing in this small
space, inches apart, his hand on her arm, the
question in his eyes and the impossible dream

of promise. One movement of her cheek, one tiny step forward and Tessa knew with a flash of absolute clarity that their lips would meet, that this was so much more than two friends getting maudlin, that the shift in tempo she'd detected hadn't been without foundation. A nervous tongue flicked across her lips and she almost felt the internal groan emanate from Max as he acknowledged the tiny gesture with his eyes.

How very easy it would have been to discard Emily from her mind, to toss away her mental image on a vague promise that their relationship was struggling, to cross the tiny space that held them apart, to say yes to dinner and excuses, but though every fibre in her being, every cell in her body screamed for his touch, she simply couldn't do it. Couldn't dip her toe in the uncharted murky waters of infidelity, couldn't tangle herself in the dark depths that had pulled her parents' marriage down.

'Better check on Josie...' His hand was still there and Tessa gave a bright smile as she reclaimed her arm and breezed past him, pushing aside the thoughts that were rampaging through her brain, her voice amazingly light given her accelerated heart rate. 'And then it's my turn for a shower.'

'We've got a problem.' Kim met Tessa at the bathroom door.

'She didn't try to get out?' Tessa asked urgently.

'No.' Kim pushed open the bathroom door. 'But there goes our morning.'

A rather remorseful-looking Josie was sitting on the hoist over the drained bath, wrapped in a mountain of white towels and covered in the white snow of talcum powder. Tessa smiled for a moment at her patient, but then, as she looked down, Tessa's mouth literally fell open, taking in the piles and wads of notes that littered the bathroom floor.

'Oh, my goodness,' Tessa said slowly, her eyes slowly scanning the bathroom floor as Josie sat there, pointedly saying nothing. 'There must be thousands of dollars here.'

'Tens of thousands, I think,' Kim said grimly. 'And it all nearly ended up in the bin. Tell her, Josie,' Kim urged in an indignant voice that surprised even Tessa. 'Tell Tessa how you were going to let me throw your coat away without telling me that you had your life savings stuffed in the lining.'

'I forgot about it,' Josie said airily, flicking her hand and turning her face away.

'She forgot about it,' Kim repeated in utter disbelief, her long initiation into emergency nursing only just starting. 'I was just about to throw her coat away when I felt something in the lining. I thought it was newspaper, you know, how you said that sometimes they stuff there clothes to keep warm? Thank goodness I checked.'

'What are you doing with all this money on you, Josie?' Tessa asked.

'I didn't steal it.'

'I'm not suggesting that you did.'

'It's my disability pension,' Josie boomed. 'I'm mentally ill, you know.'

Her twinkling eyes turned to Tessa and simultaneously a smile wobbled on both their faces and they started to giggle, a giggle that got out of hand and turned into slightly hysterical laughter.

'It's not funny, you two,' Kim scolded, stuffing the filthy money into a garbage bag with a pair of tongs. 'What the hell are we supposed to do with this lot?'

Waste an entire morning, as it turned out.

Counted, rubber-banded and sorted into neat piles under the very watchful eyes of Josie, still no decision could be reached on how best to deal with it. Josie refused to let it be put into the safe and despite Rita's, the social worker, pleas, Josie wouldn't even hear of it being banked. Technically, once the referral was made, Josie's finances ceased to be Tessa's problem, but unfortunately life was never that simple, particularly if you had a conscience. And when that conscience was coupled with a genuine affection for a seventy-something, endearingly difficult patient, it meant that the problem, for now at least, remained Tessa's.

The fact that Josie had refused all the social worker's recommendations and was completely prepared to walk out into the world with a six-figure sum in a garbage bag wasn't something Tessa felt she could just let happen in the name of patient's rights and hospital protocol.

'They'll give me one of those little plastic cards that gets eaten up.'

'You can apply for another one if that happens,' Tessa said, exasperated. 'Rita's explained all that.'

'And I won't even see my pension.'

'It will be paid in to your account directly.'

'What if I get hit over the head at the machine?'

A smart reply was on the tip of Tessa's tongue, she was starving and it was well past lunchtime, but she bit it back. Emergency nursing to the uninitiated was considered somewhat exciting, but it wasn't all high-tech drama and blood and gore. A vast amount of time was spent trying to come up with an-swers to the strangest of problems, and some-how, Tessa thought as she chewed her lip thoughtfully and eyed Josie, it wouldn't make the recruiting advertisements looks quite so exciting.

'You're more likely to be mugged, carry-ing all that money about on you. Anyway, as Rita said, you should go to supermarkets and well-lit places to use it, places where there are a lot of people around. You can even use it in shops to buy your batteries without pull-ing money out. Please, Josie, I can't just let you walk out of here with all this cash—there's enough to buy a small house here! It's just not safe.'

'Problem.' Max's calmness defused the rather tense stand-off. Tessa was exhausted, trying to reason, and Josie was sitting with her arms folded, refusing to budge an inch. 'I thought this would be sorted by now. Didn't the social worker explain everything, Josie?'

'She tried,' Tessa sighed, standing up and wincing as her knees creaked.

'Blinded me with a pile of forms more like. How am I supposed to remember a "four-digit number"? I'm—'

'Mentally ill,' Tessa finished for her. 'You don't have any trouble remembering the phone number of the radio station, Josie, and that must surely be more than four numbers.'

'It's not the same,' Josie puffed, refusing to give an inch.

'Come on, you two.' Max cocked his head and gestured towards the door. 'I'll buy you both lunch, my treat.'

Josie jumped up, followed by a reluctant Tessa. Used to Max's oddball ways by now, normally she'd have jumped like Josie at the chance for lunch with him, but right now all Tessa wanted to do was put her feet up with a mug of coffee and a magazine and read about a few Hollywood stars falling from the sky.

'We're going to lunch.' Tessa rolled her eyes as she came over to the nurses' station and handed Kim the keys as Josie wandered to the exit then stood impatiently at the swing doors, determined not to miss out on her free lunch. 'Can you give these to Jane and let her know to page me if she needs me?'

'Sure. Are you going, too, Max?'

'Yep.' Max nodded. 'And then I'm going to crash in the on call-room so, unless it's desperate, call Chris Burgess. If I don't get a couple of hours in, I'm going to be useless.'

'We're taking Josie, by the way.' Tessa scribbled on the whiteboard, a small gesture but necessary in case there was a fire or the department had to be evacuated.

'You two are terrible!' Kim laughed. 'And you both have the gall to lecture me on not getting too involved with the patients. It's just as well you're not together, your house would end up as the local drop-in centre.'

Another seemingly innocuous remark, another dose of salt in Tessa's wound. Kim looked back over to Max, who was stifling a yawn, thankfully not noticing the blush spreading across Tessa's face. 'You'd better get lunch over with, Max. You look as if you're about to fall asleep standing up.'

'I am, I've been here since three a.m. If I don't get a decent coffee soon, I think I'll keel over. Still, thank God it's Friday.' He made to go then with a jolt he turned back, a broad grin on his face.

'Ah! Thank God it's Friday,' he said again as Kim stood there smiling brightly, a big blush spreading over her face as a couple of colleagues turned around curiously. 'Can I give you a hug now your twelve weeks are up?'

'You can.' Kim half laughed, half cried. 'I'm just about to tell the world at large.'

Funny, Tessa thought to herself as the rather odd looking trio made their way along the corridor. For all Max's casual ways, for all his easygoing nature and wicked humour, there beat inside him a heart of pure gold.

A groan escaped her lips as they turned into the hospital foyer and she realised the real reason behind the little outing. Just inside the hospital canteen's foyer stood a shiny ATM.

'No way.' Tessa nudged him. 'Don't even think about it.'

But Max completely ignored her, turning instead to Josie. 'I'm going to do something I shouldn't do here,' Max warned Josie. 'I'm going to do something you must never, ever do—do you understand me?'

Josie eyed him suspiciously as Max pulled out his wallet and proceeded to tell Josie his PIN number.

'Max,' Tessa warned, but again he chose to ignore her.

'Right, Josie, put it in this slot here, that's right. Now, read the prompts.'

Tessa stood there at the ATM, quietly fuming as the hospital personnel brushed by, unable to believe Max could be so completely irresponsible, only managing a rather forced smile when a jubilant Josie turned, waving a fifty-dollar note.

'Right, you can go and get our lunch now.' Max smiled as Josie ambled off.

'That was stupid,' Tessa said angrily. 'Of all the irresponsible...'

'What's she going to do?' Max shrugged. 'Mug me? All four feet five of her?'

'You can't go around telling the patients your PIN number. What would the bank say? What would Personnel say?'

'So shoot me,' Max said easily. 'Anyway, I leave the country next week. I'll be closing the account anyway.'

'All the same,' Tessa mumbled, his imminent departure again rearing its ugly head. 'You shouldn't have done that.'

'Oh, and are you seriously trying to tell me you wouldn't have done the same if you hadn't thought of it? You're as soft as butter, Tess.'

'I wouldn't have,' Tessa insisted.

'Only because your card is probably up to its limit.' Max grinned. 'Look, the old girl was scared, all she needed was to be shown. Rita spent an entire morning confusing her when all that was needed was a trip to the ATM. It's stupid if you ask me.'

It was stupid, Tessa thought reluctantly, Maybe Social Services should think about setting up a small account for times like this, There was a genuine fear amongst the elderly and confused for anything remotely technical, and Max in his own way had cut through the red tape and dealt with the problem. But she certainly wasn't going to back down, and she certainly wasn't going to let Max know she privately agreed with him.

'Tessa.' The rather strained atmosphere was broken by the smiling face of Fred. 'I've been trying to catch up with you. Looking forward to court on Monday?'

'Don't remind me,' Tessa sighed. 'I'm trying not to think about it.' It was true. The two things Tessa was dreading were the court case and Max's departure, and both were drawing appallingly close.

'Don't get worked up, you'll be fine. I was on with you that night, remember. Nobody did anything wrong.'

'I hope not.' Tessa gestured to a chair. 'Sit down.'

But Fred shook his head. 'I'm due in Theatre, there's a full list this afternoon. Look, I just wondered if you needed a lift on Monday.'

'I'm taking her.'

It was the first time Max had spoken since Fred had joined them, and Tessa looked up at the slight edge in Max's voice.

'No worries.' Fred shrugged. 'How about lunch, then?'

Again Max jumped in before Tessa could even open her mouth. 'Better not,' Max said tersely, a distinctly proprietarial note to his voice. 'No doubt there'll be a few things we'll need to go over. It's Tessa's first time in court.'

'Fine.' Fred looked quizzically from Max to Tessa, who was sitting, mouthing like a goldfish. 'Some other time perhaps?'

The question in his voice didn't go unnoticed and for the first time in the conversation Tessa realised he was actually asking her out.

'Sure,' Tessa mumbled, her face reddening as Fred smiled and with a cheery wave walked off.

'Will you go?' Max asked when once again they were alone.

'I don't have a choice,' Tessa answered, deliberately missing the point. 'I've been summoned, remember?'

'I wasn't talking about the court case,' Max retorted sharply. 'I meant for dinner with Fred.'

'Perhaps.' Tessa shrugged, her eyes narrowing as she looked across the table. 'I really haven't given it much thought.' Still Max was looking at her. 'But why not? He seems nice enough.'

'He'd bore the hell out of you,' Max said. 'If you think all Luke talks about is work then wait till you spend an hour or two with Fred, and bear in mind his patients spend most of their time unconscious.' He rolled his eyes. 'Mind-numbing.'

Tessa's eyes were still narrowed and she stared at him thoughtfully for a moment, half cross at him for answering for her and utterly, completely confused at he way he was acting. For all the world Max Slater, Max, 'engaged with a fiancée to die for' Slater, sounded just like a jealous schoolboy.

'Bank fees!'

Slopping the coffee into the saucers, Josie slammed the tray between them and Tessa tore her eyes away as Max sat there with a defiant look on his face.

'I heard it on the radio, they charge people a fortune in bank fees.'

'Not people like you, Josie.' The jealous tinge was gone from his voice and the carefree smile was back.

'Because I'm mentally ill?' Josie asked, breaking a muffin in two.

'It's ''mentally challenged'' now, Josie,' Max smiled gently. 'And, no, it has nothing to do with that. The reason they won't charge you is because, believe it or not...' he broke into laughter as Josie looked up expectantly '...you're richer than the lot of us.'

CHAPTER FIVE

'THE diet worked, then,' Letting out a low whistle, Max followed her along the hallway of Tessa's small single-storey house, admiring her dark-stockinged legs as she clipped along the floorboards in unfamiliar high heels.

'No,' Tessa confessed. 'I took my credit card for a workout instead of myself. If I look at another egg I think I'll scream.' She gave a small laugh as she busied herself with the coffee perculator and spooned sugar and milk into mugs, not quite sure her made-up face would cover the blush that simply wouldn't fade.

'Well, you look fantastic.'

So did Max.

Of course, he wasn't going to rock up to the court in his usual fare of crumpled jeans and wild hair. But Max Slater, clean-shaven, his very newly cut hair slicked back, with just the tiniest bit of wax was a sight for sore eyes. His charcoal grey suit made the wiry body suddenly look a couple of inches taller, if that was possible, his shoulder that bit wider. Between the two of them they looked like they were heading off to a wedding or a funeral.

'I thought you said you wouldn't wear a suit for anyone,' Tessa tried to joke.

'Well, you're not just anyone.'

She should have anticipated this, Tessa mentally scolded herself. Should have realised the emotional overload having Max here in her home, looking so divine, was going to cause. So busy had she been, fretting over the court case, she hadn't prepared herself for the impact of having him here in such intimate surroundings. And it was intimate, Tessa thought, him here in her kitchen. It was a world away from the safety of work, the anonymity her uniform offered. At work, telephones rang, people rushed in and out, she was in charge and completely in control, but at home… Max had never been in her home before and having him here was having the strangest effect on Tessa. Even the scent of him was reaching her as she made heavy work of making two simple drinks.

OK, so he'd dropped her off from work a couple of times when her car had died in the car park, and once he'd had to deposit her rather unceremoniously in the hallway when the fruit punch at the Christmas party had been more than spiced up a bit. But having him in her kitchen, perched on a barstool, was causing Tessa more angst than the nine a.m. court case.

For the moment at least.

'Have you eaten?'

Tess shook her head. 'I'm not hungry for once in my life. Maybe I should get summonsed more often.' Her feeble joke went without comment, and she only finally looked around when she heard Max slamming cupboard doors. 'What are you doing?'

'I brought breakfast.' He held up a greasy paper bag. 'Chocolate croissants. If you bung them in the microwave for thirty seconds all the chocolate melts—bliss.'

'You have them,' Tessa offered, taking the bag and assembling the pastries on a plate, grateful for the diversion as he fiddled with the timer. 'I honestly couldn't eat a thing.'

Even thirty seconds seemed to go on for ever. Watching the pastries revolve aimlessly, Tessa could feel Max's eyes on her, smell his aftershave, and, though it was agony, she couldn't let the moment go without just the tiniest fantasy. The tiniest glimpse of a distant dream where breakfast with Max was a daily occurrence. And if she was dreaming, why not go the whole hog? Why not imagine that her gorgeous black suit was a daily event as well, that she was a nurse lecturer perhaps, a drug rep even? Glimpsing over to her breakfast bar where Max sat flicking through the newspaper, her fantasy took on dangerous proportions… High chairs with happy babies didn't go with corporate suits and, perhaps more to the point, fantasies involving engaged men didn't go very well with Tessa's morals.

The pastries only got a twenty-second spin.

Pinging open the door, Tessa handed the plate to Max then brought over the coffees and perched anxiously on the barstool, her teeth nibbling the skin around her thumbnail as she anxiously watched the clock.

'Tessa?'

He watched her jerk her head towards him, saw the strain in her eyes, her attempt to force a smile, and his fingers tightened hard around his coffee-cup such was the urge to go over to her to wrap his arms around her and kiss away her fears. To tell her with his touch the pride he had in her, the faith she should have in herself. And as nonchalant as Max might have looked, sitting there with the paper, he had never felt more awkward in his life. His new suit felt strange, sitting here with Tessa felt strange, hell, all he wanted to do was unburden the load from his shoulders, to tell how he was feeling. And though he'd worked his way up to this moment, though his every waking moment had been focussed on this very scenario, with no pagers, no buzzers, no patients to distract them, just him and Tessa finally alone, to see her sitting there, her face taut with anxiety, her shoulders tensed in anticipation, Max knew that the time wasn't right, that the only issue on Tessa's mind today was the court case.

'You did nothing wrong.' Max's words answered her unspoken fears and she rested her hand back down in her lap and met his confident gaze head on, wishing for all the world that she could match it. 'And today isn't about apportioning blame. The bypass issue mightn't even come into it.'

'So why are they calling me, then?'

Max gave a brief shrug. 'He was eighteen years old, Tessa. The police were involved.'

'I know all that,' Tessa responded, pushing the pastry away with a grimace. 'But this is the first time I've been called to court, and I'm sure it's not to congratulate me on my resuscitation technique. There must be a reason they want me there, and I'm sure it isn't going to be good.'

'Lets find out, shall we?' Max said, pushing his own plate away untouched, realising small talk wasn't what Tessa needed right now. 'Have you got a change of clothes?'

'Why?' Tessa asked, startled, pulling her very new and way too expensive handbag over her shoulder.

'This could very well go on until tomorrow, and unless you fancy another four-hour round trip, it might be easier to bag a room.'

'In a hotel?'

Max grinned. 'Well, I'm a bit past youth hostels. Look, I'm just thinking ahead. More than likely we'll be back here by five o'clock. I just want you to be prepared.'

Oh, Tessa was prepared all right. Prepared for the court case, prepared for two hours cooped up in a car feigning nonchalance. In fact, she was almost mentally prepared for Max's leaving party. But drinks and dinner and, heaven forbid, twin beds in some luxury hotel certainly weren't on her agenda. 'I'd rather come back here. Anyway, you really can't take two days off for me in your last week.'

'But I will.'

'I know,' Tessa answered too quickly, confused by the potential change to her plans and desperate to regain control. 'But there's really no need, no need at all. If the court case does end up going on till tomorrow, I'll at least know the ropes a bit and I'll be just fine by myself.'

'And there's always Fred to hold your hand.'

Where had that come from? That jealous tinge to his voice she had heard in the canteen was back, and this time Tessa knew she definitely wasn't hearing things. Why was he doing this? He had everything he wanted. Couldn't he just leave her heart alone?

'Yes, there's Fred,' Tessa said through slightly gritted teeth. 'But there's also a perfectly good car in my own garage. I might be blowing my own trumpet a bit here but, believe it or not, I did pass my driving test a few years back. This little lady can get to the city without a male escort. I'm not a complete hick!'

'Sorry,' Max was grinning at her outburst. 'Look, you're nervous—'

'Don't patronise me, Max.' They were standing in her hallway now, the front door wide open, and turning she saw his slightly startled expression at the testiness in her voice.

'I wasn't. Hey, Tess.' His hand catching her sleeve as she made to go was almost more contact than Tessa could bear, and biting back the sharp sting of tears she turned to face him. 'Where did this row blow in from? I just want to be here for you, I don't want you doing this alone.'

She loved him, yes. But never, not once in their five years of friendship, had she let her façade slip for even a second. Never had she given him even a glimmer of her true feelings. As far as Max was concerned, they were friends and nothing else.

Nothing else.

But suddenly Max was breaking all the rules. That fine line drawn in the sand, the line that had kept her feelings safe, kept her emotions firmly in check, was being slowly eroded. No waves gushing in, just the gentle laps of suggestion. The small proprietarial touches, the almost jealous remarks. And if all Tessa had was her dignity, she damn well wasn't going to lose it now. In five days Max Slater would be out of her life, in five days' time she wouldn't have to pretend any more. It was time to set the boundaries, make things blatantly clear, before they did something they could only both regret.

'I'm glad you're here.' Taking a deep breath, Tessa managed to look into his eyes. 'Glad that the consultant of the department is here today to back me up and guide me through.'

'I'm not here just because I'm a consultant, Tess.'

'Tessa,' she snapped. 'My name is Tessa, and if the case does drag on, I'll come with

Fred, or by myself, but either way I'll be just fine.'

'Fine,' she repeated again, reclaiming her arm and deliberately ignoring the confusion in Max's eyes at her outburst.

The sun was only just coming up as they stepped out onto the street. The city was at least a two-hour drive away and factoring peak hour traffic and the need for a last-minute coffee and pep talk Max had left plenty of time to get there. The last thing Tessa needed now was the anxiety of arriving late.

'Look at that.' As she waited for him to unlock the car their haste was put on hold as they surveyed the stunning view. The jagged golden cliffs, painted a vivid burn orange by the emerging sun, the shimmering ocean sparkling so brightly Max screwed up his eyes and shielded them with the palm of his hand. 'I'll miss all this. I doubt there's too many views like this in London.'

Tessa managed a wry grin, her anger of only moments before receding at the rate of knots as she drank in the eternally soothing view. 'Oh, I'm sure you might find a couple of things to admire there. It's London, for heaven's sake!'

'And this time next week I'll be there.'

'Freezing to death, probably,' Tessa muttered, pulling impatiently on the locked car door.

Maybe it was for the best, Tessa mused as the car ate up the miles. There were definite undercurrents. Oh, she didn't for a second believe that he loved her, but maybe, despite her best efforts, the attraction she felt was starting to show, however subliminally. And maybe Max wasn't quite the hero she'd believed. Perhaps his morals didn't quite stand up to the test of time and the emotion of leaving.

He was male after all.

Tessa pretty much knew what to expect when she got to court, and not just from Max.

Endless colleagues had gone over their own experiences, offered her their unlimited support, but the woodwork that adorned the room had, in Tessa's mind, been grander, more ornate perhaps, certainly not the modern cherry-wood that greeted them, and the pale carpets and modern furnishings were a revelation in themselves. Still, the absence of robes or wigs and the contemporary surroundings did nothing to detract from the reverence of the occasion, and the hushed tones that swept the rapidly filling room were pretty much in keeping with Tessa's image.

But all the preparation, all the forewarnings didn't prepare Tessa for the stab of pain she felt when she saw Matthew's parents, sitting in the front row, holding each other's hands, the lines on their faces new, the etchings of grief so clearly visible they looked as if they had been painted on, wearing the stiff upper lip of bereaved parents that belied the pained torturous nights, the horror of living in a world that carried on without their baby.

But today the world did pause for a moment, here in the surroundings of the court the last hours of Matthew Benton's life were examined gently yet astutely by the coroner. The packed room listened intently to the endless reports, the reams of witnesses and officers' findings, and Tessa listened intently, breathing an audible sigh of relief along with Max and the rest of the court when Matthew's blood and drug screen readings were relayed. Documented proof that for once the fatal combination of teenage egos and alcohol hadn't played a part in this accident.

Small comfort, Tessa thought, looking over at Matthew's parents, watching Mr Benton's grip tighten on his wife's hand, a small proud smile flickering on his lips. But, Tessa mused as she watched the struggling couple, when you've lost a son, you'll take any comfort on offer.

Stepping outside at lunchtime, Tessa took a deep cleansing breath. It was like coming out of a bizarre movie or a play, she thought, blinking at the bright midday sun, and so hard to fathom that the people bustling past on the street were untouched by the events unfolding in the courtroom behind her.

'Where do you want to go for lunch?' Max's voice broke into her thoughts and Tessa turned her troubled face to him.

'I'm not hungry.'

'Come on, Tess, you haven't eaten anything all day.'

'I'm going to be called soon, Max. I'm so nervous that I honestly think I'll throw up if I eat. Sorry,' Tessa added. 'That wasn't very ladylike.'

'I'm shocked,' Max feigned a stunned expression, then smiled. 'You need a break, Tessa. There's a nice little bistro over the street, I've booked us a table.'

'You've already booked?' The doubts that had plagued Tessa earlier that morning seemed to be rapidly returning for an encore. 'Well, you shouldn't have,' Tessa responded hotly. 'Anyway, I need to disappear for an hour.'

'Why?'

'I can't say. I really need to get as far away from this courtroom as possible and not think about it for a while. Look, I'll meet you back here in half an hour.'

'You know I'll only follow you,' Max insisted, deliberately ignoring her angry tones. 'Come on, tell me, where are you going?'

Tessa shuffled on the spot, her feet in agony in her shoes. 'Use your imagination.'

He stared at her, bemused.

'Who's the only one in the department who ever thinks to set up a collection when's someone's leaving? Who's the mug who spends her lunch-break trying to work out how to make fifty dollars look like a hundred?'

Max laughed. 'Did you only manage to collect fifty dollars for me?'

'On the contrary, for once people were only too happy to chip in.'

'Probably glad to see the back of me.'

'Something like that.'

It was so much easier to joke.

'So what are you going to get me?' Max asked with a cheeky wink. 'Have you been picking up the hints I've been dropping?'

'You've been dropping hints?' Tessa looked up, alarmed. 'Well, I wouldn't be counting on me getting them. I'm useless at reading between the lines.'

'Tell me about it,' Max murmured, then smiled again. 'I haven't been dropping hints. The truth is, I haven't even thought about a leaving present, but now that you mention it... Come on, Tess, you know I hate surprises.'

'Well, I was going to get you a fountain pen, a nice pen with your name engraved on it.'

'I'd only lose it,' he pointed out.

'You'd better not, Max.' Fishing the envelope out of her bag, she showed it to him, watching his eyes widen as he read the figure Tessa had faithfully written on the front. 'You're going to get a pen set. Ballpoint, fountain and, if there's enough money left after that, we might even throw in a pencil.'

'Those ones that snap the lead if you push too hard.'

'The very same.' Tessa smiled. 'You can choose, but tell anyone and I'll kill you.'

They wandered off to Myers department store, the scent of the perfumery knocking them sideways as they entered the store.

'Ooh, look.' Tessa picked up a massive bottle and breathed in deeply, accepting the assistant's offer of a sprayed card, which she put in her bag. 'Remind me to get another one on my way out.'

'Why?' Max asked, following behind. 'What do you want with two pieces of cardboard?'

'One to make my bag smell nice, one for my jumper drawer. Simple.'

'Women.' Max shrugged.

Tessa had naïvely thought you walked in, chose a pen you liked and then paid for it.

Wrong!

There were hundreds, literally hundreds to choose from and, as the rather alarmingly knowledgeable sales assistant pointed out, colour was just a tiny consideration.

Tiny.

Gold nibs, stainless-steel nibs, different widths, different weights, did sir use his left hand, right hand, or was he perhaps ambidextrous?

'It's worse than trying to get life insurance,' Tessa muttered as the assistant unlocked yet another display cabinet.

'I'm having a ball,' Max enthused. 'I think I've got a buried pen fetish. Look at this one. Black, sleek, nice size.'

'It's a pen, Max, not a sports car!'

'I love it.' Max held it in his hands, turned it over and weighed it between his fingers as the sales assistant cooed like a dove. 'I'm serious—I adore it. Is there enough for this one?'

'If I buy a really crappy card and you forgo a bow.'

'Done.'

'And you'd better not lose it!'

'Scout's honour.'

'You're very spoiled,' the assistant gushed, lovingly placing the set in a velvet box. 'I hope you're going to get your girlfriend something nice in return.'

'She doesn't deserve it.' Max winked, tossing a playful arm around Tessa, not bothering to put the assistant right.

And for a tiny slice of time it was nice to pretend.

Pretend they were just another couple, buying a gift. A brief happy interlude in an otherwise awful day.

But all too soon it was over, all too soon they were back in court, and Tessa's moment of truth edged ever closer. The inquiry moved to the hospital and though it must have been agony for Matthew's parents, they declined the coroner's offer to leave for a while as the more gruesome details were read out. Instead, they sat in a strained, dignified silence as the post-mortem findings were detailed and the paramedics and then Fred relayed their part in the end of Matthew's short life.

'Just speak the truth.' Max gripped her hand as Tessa's name was called, and for once she didn't pull away. At this moment she needed his strength, needed the comfort of his touch.

Taking the bible, Tessa thought she was in a strange dream. She had seen scenes like this on the television but there was no comfort in false reality, her voice wavering as she recited her name, then later answered the coroner's questions as truthfully as she could, every memory of that fateful night etched on her brain, allowing for total recall.

'Why did you put the department on bypass?'

'We were busy,' Tessa ventured. 'I had a child in Resus with suspected meningococcal, and we'd taken two victims already from this accident. There were also a lot of other sick patients in the cubicles. When I heard there were two more trapped at the scene I informed the doctor in charge and we decided to go on bypass.'

'But Matthew arrived anyway.'

Tessa nodded but, realising an answer was called for, leant towards the microphone. 'Yes. It normally takes twenty minutes to half an hour for the bypass system to be put into place.'

She braced herself for some sharp questions, for some loaded legal jargon, for them to berate her lack of foresight, yet it never came.

'So you were aware, when you made that call, that more patients could still arrive?'

'Yes,' Tessa said simply.

She was speaking the truth.

For an age the coroner peered at his notes before returning his shrewd gaze to her. 'Dr Frederick Atkins states that all care was delivered to Matthew, that there were sufficient staff to deliver an effective resuscitation. Would you agree, Sister?'

'Yes. When Matthew arrived I arranged for the immediate transfer of the child with meningococcal to Intensive Care. The other victims from the accident had stabilised.'

'So you were able to deal with Matthew efficiently?'

'I believe so,' Tessa answered quietly, and though it was the truth, though she knew nothing different could have been done, there was something else she needed to say. Leaning forward slightly, she looked at the coroner. 'However...' Her voice shook. This wasn't something she had prepared in her endless rounds of talks with the hospital's solicitor. 'As efficiently as I feel we dealt with Matthew, I don't believe his parents were afforded the level of care they deserved. As I said, we were exceptionally busy that night. I wish I could have spent more time with them, been able to impart how sorry we were.'

Her eyes flicked to the couple who nodded briefly back at her. Though she had dreaded this day, wished with all her heart that it wouldn't happen, finally she realised its importance, the need for some form of closure, a chance for introspection and hopefully somewhere along the way acceptance. Tessa was eternally grateful that she had had her say, conveyed to the Bentons her sorrow for their pain.

'Thank you, Sister.'

And then it was over.

For Tessa at least.

The policeman who spoke next looked younger than her, and Tessa realised was just as nervous, his voice unsteady.

It affects us all, Tessa thought with a start.

The firefighters, the paramedics, the police officers, the doctors—even Fred with his endless nonchalance had been hesitant when he'd spoken, his voice breaking for a tiny second as he'd met the parents' eyes.

Life was precious and they all fought in their own small way to guard it.

Max held her hand as the coroner summed up his findings and Tessa, who usually cried at the drop of a hat, determinedly held the tears back. This day was for Matthew, for his parents. So she listened as he spoke of the tragic end to Matthew's life, his comments directed compassionately at the parents, no blame being apportioned for there was none. It had been, as the coroner said, a tragic accident.

'Feel better?'

The hand that had held hers in court was still there, and Tessa gripped it tightly as she stepped out into the late afternoon sun.

'I think so,' she admitted. 'I was expecting objections and cross-examinations, and for everything I said to be jumped on and dissected, but in the end I hardly said anything...'

'You said the one thing that mattered.' She was facing Max now listening as his insight yet again floored her. 'That's what you've been beating yourself up about, isn't it? The fact you didn't have the time to spend with Matthew's parents.'

Tessa nodded. 'It's an important part of nursing. Matthew's care shouldn't have stopped just because he died.'

'I know you, Tessa, and I bet you weren't sitting in the coffee-room, having a break, were you?'

She shook her head and opened her mouth to speak, but Max got there first.

'And I'd lay my last dollar on the fact that the time you did manage to spend with his parents, however short, however fleeting, was compassionate and professional.'

She nodded almost reluctantly.

'It's over,' Max said softly.

'For us maybe,' Tessa sighed, tears filling in her eyes as she watched Matthew's parents come out of the courtroom, Mr Benton's arm wrapped protectively around his wife who clung to her husband's arm like she was drowning. 'But it will never be over for them.'

'You can't be everywhere, Tessa, you can't spread yourself that thin, no matter how much you want to.'

'I know that.' Tessa managed a feeble smile. 'Thin is something I'll never be.'

'Come on, I want to show you something.' Still his hand was there and, walking through the five o'clock crowd, they wandered to the

Rialto, Tessa frowning as they pushed the revolving doors and Max bought two tickets.

'Why are you taking me to the observation deck? You know I hate heights.'

The lift moved fast and suddenly they were on the top of the world, or the top of Melbourne at least. They bypassed the café, Max walking purposefully to the windows. He stood there and she joined him, wrapping an arm around her shoulders as they stood in mutual silence, gazing down on the streets far below, their eyes slowly following the Yarra River coiling through the city, the MCG, the Tennis Centre all on show.

'You can't solve all the world's problems, Tessa,' Max said finally. 'It all looks so beautiful yet it's just an overview. There's a lot of breaking hearts down there, there are too many Josies and Matthews in the world, too many people swimming against the tide, doing it tough. But from up here you can almost believe life's easy.'

I'm going,' he said after the longest pause, and the tears that had been held back all day started to trickle down Tessa's cheeks as Max carried on talking. 'And it sounds so straightforward, so damned easy—a dream job, only a year. I've said it so many times I'm almost starting to believe it myself.'

'Almost?'

He wasn't looking at her. His eyes were staring vacantly at the stunning view but he nodded slightly at her perception. 'I don't want to go, Tessa.'

'Then don't.' Wiping her cheeks with the back of her hand, Tessa found her voice.

'It's not that simple.' A long ragged sigh dragged out of his lips, his hand ran impatiently through his hair, yet no further explanation came.

'Maybe it is that simple,' Tessa ventured.

'You don't understand.'

'Then tell me, explain to me why you're going to the other side of the world when you so clearly don't want to. You've got everything you could need here, Max. A job you adore, a whole community that you're such a big part of. A fiancée you love.' She swallowed hard, hating to admit it but knowing it to be true. 'So if you're having doubts, if you've changed your mind, do something about it. There's no shame in admitting that you were wrong, that you've decided not to go. They'll withdraw your notice in a flash...'

'It's too late for that.'

'It isn't,' Tessa urged. 'It's your life, Max, yours, and you should follow your heart and just do what it is you really want.'

Was it an opening? Had she deep down instigated what happened next? Tessa truly didn't know. The one thing she knew for sure as Max turned, as his lips moved towards her, as the line she had so carefully drawn disintegrated into nothing, was that she needed this kiss, wanted Max more than she had ever wanted anything. And as his lips brushed hers, as his arms wrapped around her, pulling her towards him with an urgency that matched her desire, for a second or two nothing else mattered, nothing other than this precious, stolen, beautiful moment, where morality was suspended in the name of passion, where good intentions were waved away in a flash of impulse. And as sweet as it was, as natural as his lips felt on hers, as breathtaking as the passion that bubbled between them was, as his chin grazed her cheeks, as he pressed his body closer with aching clarity, reality invaded, Tessa's blissfully closed eyes snapping open in horror, the enormity of what had taken place suffocating her.

Pushing him away, she shook her head blindly. 'You shouldn't have done that,' she gasped. '*We* shouldn't have done that.' Blinking back tears, her mind reeled for comfort, for an explanation, for justification, but there was none. Nothing, *nothing* could justify what had just taken place, what Max had just done.

What Tessa had so willingly let him do.

'Tessa, please...'

'Please, what?' Her voice was rising now, angry tears coursing down her cheeks.

'Let me explain.' He was holding her arm, holding it tightly, his eyes pleading for her to stay, to calm down.

'Explain what? That you didn't mean for it to happen? That it was an accident, just a kiss? No harm done?' People were looking now, placing their coffee-cups in their saucers and nudging each other, half embarrassed, half curious, but Tessa couldn't have cared less.

'I love you Tessa.'

The world stopped for a moment, quiet and still, as the words that had filled her dreams finally found their place in reality. But her dreams had been sweet and pure, not this soiled, muddied offering. She knew he was lying, using those beautiful words to right their wrong. Maybe that was what fuelled her, made it easy to impart the biggest lie of her life.

'Well, I don't love you, Max.' She saw a flash of pain in his eyes but deliberately ignored it. 'You're a friend, just a friend, and you took advantage of me being emotional.'

'Tess…'

'Tessa,' she bit back. 'It's Tessa.' Her eyes were almost jumping out with fury. 'And you're way out of line.'

'It's over between Emily and I.'

It was a crumb, a tiny crumb of comfort but Tessa was too suspicious and too scared to take it at face value.

'So can I tell the world we're on, Max? Can I go back to work on Thursday and let them know that we're together?'

'No, but—'

'Can I at least check the facts with Emily?' She stood there with a pained dignity as he shook his head.

'Then it's not over, Max.'

'Why does it all have to be so black and white to you, Tessa? These are emotions we're dealing with, feelings—can't you understand it's not always that simple?'

'It is that simple, Max, at least it is to me.' Her anger numbed the pain, enough at least for a dignified exit. 'And I hate you for lying to me.'

'Tessa.' His voice was a raw shout and he grabbed at her wrist, spinning her around and jerking her face towards him. 'This is me,

Max. I'm not your father, I'm not out to hurt you. I'm not out to hurt anyone.'

'Maybe not.' Her voice was so choked that when it came Max had to strain to listen. 'But I'm not my mother either, and I'm certainly not going to let myself be like the damn woman who's made her life hell!' Wrenching her arm away, she turned on her heel, somehow managing to hold things together all the way to the lift, banging the 'close' button furiously as Max slammed at the door, biting back the tears as the lift plummeted down, her heart left behind with her stomach. Tears blinded her as she stepped out onto the street, stunned that the traffic was still moving, that people were walking hand in hand, buying papers, rushing for their trams, when her world had just disintegrated.

'Tessa.'

Jumping back, she watched as Fred slid to a halt, hanging his head out of the car window.

'Where's Max?'

'He met up with some friends from uni.' How easily the lies rolled off her tongue, how sordid the world of underground love would be. 'I'm not up to socialising. I thought I might head home.'

Cars were tooting behind Fred as he held up the traffic, impatient drivers wanting to get home to their families, to their loved ones and children, to their straightforward lives. She was sure Fred must surely know that she was lying, must somehow be able to guess what had just taken place. Her lips were still stinging from their brief kiss and she was sure that the guilt in her eyes must read like a newspaper headline. 'Any chance of that lift home?'

She jumped in just as Max stepped out of the Rialto. Frustrated and impatient, he hurtled onto to the street, his hungry eyes scanning the crowd. Clicking on her seat belt, she managed a half-smile at Fred before her eyes turned back and locked with Max's.

It would have been so easy to do something reckless here, to poke out her tongue or sneer distastefully, but somehow it didn't seem enough.

If he did love her, if Max truly cared, there was one thing that would hurt him more than anything. With a dismissive toss of her head, Tessa turned, dazzling the side of Fred's unseeing head with the most charming of smiles.

Let him look, Tessa thought with a strange surge of triumph, let him feel a tenth of the pain he's inflicted on me.

Fred was actually good company.

Nice, funny, good-looking, successful, everything a girl could want.

If only she loved him.

But Tessa didn't love him, and playing with someone's emotions after the cruel blow she had just been dealt wasn't exactly on the top of her list. In fact, by the time the car had pulled off from the traffic lights and Max was a blur in the rear-view mirror, Tessa had declined an offer of dinner and had made it very clear that friends was all they were going to be.

Male friends, Tessa thought ruefully. I could write a book on it.

Getting out of the city took for ever with banked-up peak-hour traffic, but at least the evening glare of the sun gave Tessa an excuse to wear her sunglasses, and the busy road kept conversation pretty light.

And as confused as Tessa was, as utterly perplexed as she felt, there was one thing of which she was certain.

Max wasn't going to leave things there. He'd be on her doorstep with in minutes of her getting home and right now Max Slater was the very last person Tessa wanted to see.

'Actually, Fred, can I change my mind? I think I might head off to my mum's, she's only a few minutes away from here.'

'Can't say I blame you,' Fred said easily as he followed her instructions, bypassing the freeway and following instead the winding beach road along the bay. 'You've had a rough day. A good dose of TLC sounds in order.'

'Do you want a coffee?' Tessa offered, trying and failing not to sound too half-hearted with her offer as they pulled up outside the pretty weatherboard house, the tubs of flowers on the veranda drooping listlessly in the early evening sun, the sprinklers spluttering into life as she pulled open the passenger door. But Fred just gave his lazy smile, not remotely fazed at her eagerness to get inside.

'Better not.'

For someone who cried so easily, Tessa did amazingly well—not a single tear slid under her glasses, she even managed a wave from her parents' front door. But as soon as the front door was pulled open, as soon as the smiling, trusting face of her mother greeted her, her façade dissolved so rapidly that for a second Mrs Hardy thought someone must surely have died.

CHAPTER SIX

ASSERTIVENESS was never Tessa's forte.

Sure, at work she could make snap decisions, delegate, even relegate when she had to, but when it came to matters of the heart it was a different situation altogether. How Tessa would have loved to have headed to her own home, to calmly open the door when Max undoubtedly appeared with his attempt at explanation. To listen to him coolly, disdainfully even, before shrugging him off with some crushing reply.

Fat chance.

A far more realistic scenario was Tessa bursting into tears on impact, and apologising for storming off. Max Slater was comparable to chocolate—infinitely desirable, desperately craved but, unfortunately, terribly bad for you.

And her will-power around him was zero.

Far more terrifying, though, than the thought of confrontation was the awful gnawing truth that, despite her morals, despite her abhorrence of an affair, the very real chance she would given in to the temptation that overwhelmed her at times, accept his excuses, accept his explanation and tumble into bed with him.

Start the diet tomorrow, so to speak.

For that tiny glimpse of paradise, the bliss of his lips on hers, the intimacy of his kiss, had Tessa utterly and completely lost.

Her days off were spent instead skulking in her old bedroom, taking long walks on the same beach she normally frequented, just fifty or so kilometres further along, and, while hating herself for it, tucking into the mountains of comfort food her mum lined the cupboards and fridges with. Anyway, Tessa consoled herself as she poured warm milk over some cereal and spooned on the sugar, she was hardly going to drop a lot of weight in her two days off. And more to the point, looking good for Max wasn't on her agenda.

'Why not ring in sick?' Bronwyn Hardy placed a steaming mug of hot chocolate in front of her daughter, perhaps not the most nutritious breakfast drink but it filled a hole, an aching, gaping hole.

Temporarily at least.

'Because I'm not sick,' Tessa said, taking a sip of the steaming drink. Lovesick maybe, but she didn't fancy her chances of asking Dr Hays, the family GP, to write that on a medical certificate. 'Well, have you thought about what I said last night?' Bronwyn pulled up a chair at the kitchen table and put the teatowel she was holding down in front of her, clearly settling in for another heart to heart.

'There's nothing to think about. What time are you going to the hairdresser's?'

'Not until two.' Bronwyn gave her a shrewd smile. 'And don't try and change the subject.'

'I'm not, Mum,' Tessa lied. 'I just don't need to think about it. I'm not going to leave Peninsula Hospital. Why would I when I love my job?'

'I know you do, dear,' Bronwyn reasoned. 'But it *is* a stressful job, and you seem to bring home all the worries with you. How many times have you fretted over a patient, and not just the sick ones either? You're always worrying about the homeless, and the like. It's bound to catch up sooner or later. What you need is a break, a proper one. Lots of young people take a year out and travel these days.'

'I'm hardly a teenager.'

'So? Look, Tessa, I've never seen you so upset. I know you don't want to talk about the inquest, but I know it's affected you deeply. You've been worrying about it for months. Look at how much weight you've lost!'

'And look at how much weight I still need to lose,' Tessa pointed out. 'I'm hardly fading away with worry.'

Tessa hated lying, hated the fact her mum was so worried about her and that she had let her think it was all tied up with the inquest, that her tears and later melancholy were all somehow work-related. But how could she tell her mother the truth after all she had been through with her own marriage? Sure, after the initial shock, Tessa didn't doubt her mum would support her, go right on loving her, but seeing the disappointment in her eyes was something Tessa just couldn't deal with right now.

'Just think about it, Tessa,' Bronwyn carried on unmercifully. 'You could travel around Europe like your cousin Sally, get a job in London even. Isn't where that consultant you work with is heading off to? Perhaps he could put in a good word for you, you're a great nurse.'

'Mum, leave it, please.'

'No, Tessa, I won't leave it,' Bronwyn insisted, misinterpreting the blush on her daughter's face. 'Why shouldn't he put in word for you? What's so good about the London hospitals that they won't take a good Australian nurse? And if Mac can get your foot in the door, why not seize the day?'

'His name's Max,' Tessa said, furiously filling her bowl again from the box of cereal in front of her. 'And the last thing I need right now is to be grovelling to him for favours.'

'But, Tessa...' Bronwyn's voice trailed off as her daughter shot a look across the breakfast table.

'I'm not going anywhere,' Tessa said sharply. Too sharply, she realised as she watched her mother blink back a few tears—the leaking tear ducts were obviously hereditary. 'Mum, I'm fine, really I am. I just needed to check out for a couple of days, to be spoiled and mollycoddled, and I'm sorry for all the worry I've caused you, but there really isn't a problem, I'm great now.'

'Honestly?'

'Honestly,' Tessa lied, making her way around the table and giving her mum a hug. 'Anyway, why on earth would I want to go to London? You know how much I hate the cold.'

'That's true,' Bronwyn sniffed.

'And you'd miss me.' Tessa managed a grin and a playful nudge. 'Remember how you embarrassed me at the airport when I went to Queensland for a fortnight.'

'You were much younger then.'

'I was twenty-two.' Tessa straightened up. 'You're stuck with me, Mum, so no more talk about backpacking holidays and big London hospitals.'

'But you'll be all right?' Bronwyn still wasn't quite convinced. She'd seen Tessa down, had heard her break her heart over patients, had nursed her through a couple of broken romances when Tessa had sworn her heart would never mend, but never, not once in twenty-nine years of mothering, had she seen the pain she had witnessed in Tessa when she had arrived utterly bereft at her doorstep two nights ago.

'I'll be just fine,' Tessa said assuredly. Picking up her bag, she slung it over her shoulder. 'I'd best head off home and dig out my uniform, and you've got to get ready. Look, stop worrying about me. It's your thirty-first wedding anniversary today. You should be painting your nails and fretting about what to wear, not getting worked up over your cranky daughter. So, where's Dad taking you for your anniversary?'

'Just a little seafood restaurant on the bay. We used to go there when we first started dating.'

'It sounds lovely.'

As her mum dashed off to answer the telephone, Tessa gulped down the last of her chocolate, determined to say goodbye to her mum with the brightest of smiles.

'I *really* am OK, Mum,' she said as Bronwyn came back into the kitchen, but seeing her mum's strained face, the smile faded in an instant. 'Who was that on the phone?'

'Your father.' Bronwyn picked up the tea-towel and flicked it across a couple of plates, but her shaking shoulders let Tessa know what was coming next. 'He has to fly off to Sydney tonight, seems they've called him for an early breakfast meeting tomorrow.'

'But it's your wedding anniversary,' Tessa said. 'He can't do this to you today. I'm going to ring him, tell him to cancel—'

'Leave it, Tessa.' There was a warning note to Bronwyn's voice that stopped Tessa midway to the telephone. 'It's only our thirty-first, it's not exactly a milestone one, we can go out and celebrate at the weekend.'

'So long as something doesn't come up,' Tessa muttered.

'Don't start, Tessa,' Bronwyn warned. 'Your father's not happy about it, but it's his work, it's not as if he has any choice in the matter.'

'Doesn't he?'

Tessa's question hung in the air unanswered as Bronwyn gave a small shrug and turned back to the sink, effectively dismissing her daughter.

'You'd better get moving, Tessa.' Bronwyn's voice was unnaturally high as she forced an air of cheerfulness, an act she had perfected well over the years. 'There's some sandwiches cut for you in the fridge—best ham, and I managed to get some of that pickle you like.'

'You'll be all right, Mum?' Tessa checked gently. 'I mean, I *can* ring in sick if you want me to stay.'

'Don't be daft,' Bronwyn said.

'The place won't collapse without me.'

'And neither will I.' Bronwyn kissed her cheek and even managed a watery smile. 'Go to work, Tessa, I'd really rather be on my own for now.'

Home was just as she'd left it.

No banners flying outside, warning of the scarlet woman that resided there, no broken windows or neighbours shaking their fists.

It was just a kiss, Tessa checked herself, mocking her own imagination.

He said he loved you. That stalled her in the hallway, but only momentarily.

He'd no doubt said the same to Emily.

The answering machine flickering away Tessa had braced herself for but the second she deleted the unheard messages, she regretted it. His voice, his explanation lost for ever, erased.

If only she could rewind to Monday, freeze-frame the moment that they'd sat on the barstools, still just as friends. If only she could somehow have foreseen what was to come, what would she have done different?

Had she been flirting at the department store, should she have corrected the sales assistant? Refused to go up to the observation deck? Staring distractedly out of the window, Tessa put a shaking hand to her lips.

No.

Because that would take away the one sweet moment in this whole sorry mess.

Max's kiss.

One kiss wasn't a lot to show for five years of love, but it was almost worth the pain.

Almost.

Two more days to get through, two days of smiling and laughing, two more shifts plus his leaving lunch and finally the party.

In the days leading up to the inquest the days had peeled away, the calendar racing by like a film where they'd happily moved to the next month. Yet now the hands of time seemed to have stopped. Every hour, every moment a feat in itself. Hiding at her mother's had been necessary and nice, but now it was time to face the music.

'Did you enjoy your days off?' Jane didn't even bother to look up from the whiteboard as Tessa approached, her greeting so wooden, so uncomfortable that Tessa's already reddened face deepened its colour.

'Not bad.'

'Max said the court case went all right, you must be so relieved.' She turned around awkwardly, not looking Tessa in the eye.

'What's the problem, Jane?' Whatever was coming, Tessa was ready for it. Sleepless nights had been filled trying to work out how to best deal with the infamous hospital grapevine, and she had decided that any gossip would be nipped in the bud right here and right now.

'I've got a wry neck,' Jane sighed.

'Sorry?'

'I woke up with it. The twins climbed into bed with us and I spent half the night hanging over the side of the bed and now I can't move.'

Tessa was so relieved she almost laughed then smothered it with a cough.

'I shouldn't have come in, or at the very least I should have taken a taxi,' Jane carried on abstractedly. 'You should try looking left then right then left again when your neck's frozen. I just about killed myself getting here.'

'Leave the car here tonight,' Tessa offered. 'I'll see if I can rustle up a cab charge from Heather.'

'Some chance!' Jane huffed.

'Well, then, I'll drop you home—you can't risk having an accident. Are you sure you're all right to work today, Jane?' Tessa's heart sank at the thought of calling for yet another agency nurse. They were short-staffed as it was without calling in someone who didn't even know the department.

'I'm going to have to be,' Jane said in a martyred voice. 'Ella called in sick so we're already down on numbers. I'll just have to battle on as best I can.'

Battle being the operative word.

The late shift started off easily enough. All the patients were pretty straightforward, and there was easily enough work to keep Max and Tessa safely at arm's length, but no sooner had Tessa returned from coffee to send the early shift home that the rumblings started.

'Didn't you get my messages?'

Max, who she'd been so skilfully avoiding, caught Tessa unawares as she stripped a trolley in one of the recently vacated cubicles.

'What messages?'

'Oh, come on, Tessa. I must have rung ten times. I've been so worried.'

'Worried?' Her voice was tinged with the incredulous grin he couldn't see as she busied herself, tucking in a sheet. 'Worried I might say the wrong thing? Worried I might land you in hot water with Emily?'

'I've been worried about *you*.' That didn't even bring a response as Tessa plunged a large plastic pillow into a rather small pillowcase. 'The last I saw, you were getting into a car with Fred and you haven't been home for two days.'

He waited for an answer, a response, in the end reverting to impatiently pulling the pillow from Tessa and hurling it onto the trolley. 'Will you, please, answer me, Tessa?'

'I wasn't aware you'd asked a question,' Tessa answered cheekily. 'In fact, even if you had, I don't think it really deserves a reply. Not even my own mother asks for an itinerary of my movements so I hardly think I'm answerable to my boss. I had two days off, in case you hadn't noticed.'

'I've been worried,' he intoned.

'Why? Did you think Fred had kidnapped me? Whisked me off to have his wicked way? I'm a big girl, Max, some might say too big. I can look after myself, thank you very much.'

'I knew you were upset. We needed to talk.'

'Wrong on both counts.' Tessa faked a smile. 'I'm not upset, and we most definitely don't need to talk.'

'Sorry, guys.' Jane was too preoccupied with her neck to notice the strained atmosphere. 'We're filling up outside and a we've just had a storm warning passed through.'

'I'll be right there.' Grateful for the excuse Tessa made to go, but Max pulled her back.

'Tessa…'

'If you were that worried about me,' Tessa said with a calm logic that defied her pounding heart, 'then you should just have asked Fred.' Again she made to go, but this time it was Tessa that stopped. Tessa that turned back with a black look on her face. 'But you couldn't do that, could you? Couldn't risk making Fred suspicious. It must have been a rotten couple of days for you, mustn't it, Max? Wondering what I'd told him, wondering if you were about to be knocked off the pedestal this department's put you on. Don't worry, I'm not about to shatter anyone's illusions. You can go away with them all thinking you're the nice guy you so perfectly portray. One word of advice, though.' She shot him a sweet smile that clearly didn't meet her eyes. 'You mightn't be so lucky next time.'

'Next time?' Max stared at her bemused.

'Oh, there'll be a next time,' Tessa said darkly. 'Not with me, but if you can't manage to be faithful now, what hope have you got in London? Emily's not a fool, Max, and she'll see through you soon enough.'

The waiting room had filled as quickly as the black clouds in the sky. Stretchers were coming in through Triage, the paramedics drenched as they relayed their findings.

'Darren Canning, forty-two, coming home from work and lost control of the car on the freeway,' Ryan, Tessa's favourite paramedic, said in his booming Australian accent. 'He's got multiple superficial abrasions and a nasty seat-belt injury. There's probably a couple of fracture ribs there,' Ryan added. 'Some cars slammed into the back of him so there's a few more heading your way, Tessa.'

'Are any of them seriously injured?'

Thankfully, Ryan, shook his head. 'Not at this stage, but we'll be tied up there a while.'

'Hi, Darren.' Tessa smiled gently. 'How are you feeling at the moment?'

'Like a fool.' Darren mumbled, his shocked face as white as the bandage tightly wrapped around his forehead. 'I wasn't even going that fast.'

'It wasn't your fault, mate,' Ryan said quickly, and though it seemed like an empty statement for the paramedic to be making it. Tessa knew it must be true. He wouldn't give that kind of reassurance if it wasn't genuine. 'The roads are like glass out there. All this rain after a long dry spell is lethal.'

'Let's get you onto a trolley, shall we?' Darren wasn't exactly dressed for easy access. His suit and tie, combined with his newly fractured ribs, proved a struggle even for Tessa, who had boasted for a giggle at a nurses' night out that she could undress most men in two minutes flat.

'Need a hand?' Kim offered.

'Thanks, Kim.' Tessa smiled at her colleague standing in the cubicle entrance, massaging her back as if she were eight months pregnant instead of twelve weeks. 'Are you OK?'

'I'm fine,' Kim said assuredly, but Tessa was convinced she was putting on a brave face. Despite her apparent legendary morning sickness, coupled with a bladder the size of a thimble, Kim had soldiered on without a word of complaint, and now she was standing pinched and pale-looking and obviously in some discomfort.

'If you need a break, I'll manage on my own,' Tessa offered, but her kind words only seemed to upset Kim.

'I'm fine, Tessa,' she snapped uncharacteristically. 'What do you want me to do?'

'If you could finish getting Darren undressed and run a set of obs, that would be great,' Tessa replied easily, ignoring Kim's snappish response, her mind filled with more important matters. 'I'm just going to make a phone call.'

As she made her way to the telephone, the fateful night when Matthew had died played over and over in Tessa's mind. OK, Tessa reasoned, everyone had said she was blameless, even the coroner, and the care Matthew had received had been appropriate for his injuries, no doubt about that. But if Matthews death had taught Tessa anything, it was never to be too proud to ask for help.

And ask in time.

Jane, with her wry neck, should be at home with a hot pack, Kim clearly wasn't a hundred per cent, and though Tessa had a few other nursing staff on duty with her, their experience didn't add up to much. The foreboding skies and the paramedic's words needed to be heeded. At any moment the place could ignite, and with the staff Tessa had on she wasn't quite sure they would handle it. But as Tessa voiced her very real concerns into the telephone, the nursing supervisor begged to differ.

'I know we're not *exceptionally* busy,' Tessa said somewhat exasperatedly, even rolling her eyes and managing a half-smile as Max entered, the drumming of the rain loud against the darkened windows. 'But the department is filling and I could really use an extra staff member just to clear some patients to the wards and fetch and carry.' A rather prolonged exchange followed as Tessa was given a guided tour of the department's failure to meet its budget and the staff-patient ratios deemed appropriate by the nameless faces in Admin. 'All of which I understand,' Tessa said as diplomatically as she could, 'but you know how quickly things change down here.'

'Let me try,' Max offered, and, as proud she was, Tessa wasn't going to jeopardise the patients.

'Max Slater here, Sister.' His voice was affable, but there was no mistaking the authority behind it. 'Sister Hardy is concerned with the safety levels down here and frankly so am I. We're in for one helluva evening so two more staff would be much appreciated.'

'Two?' The splutter down the phone was audible even to Tessa.

'For now,' Max replied easily 'If that number goes up, I'll be sure to let you know.

'They're on their way.' He grinned as he hung up the telephone.

'Thanks for that.'

'I had an ulterior motive. Now you've no excuse not to take your supper break later.' He was smiling but the confidence in his voice had gone now that the conversation had moved to a more personal level and Tessa could feel herself start to weaken. Maybe she should hear what Max had to say about the other evening, should at least give him the benefit of the doubt until she heard his explanation.

This was Max.

Her friend.

Five years of friendship had to count for something.

As if sensing her weakness, God, or the powers that be, threw in a firecracker, nothing too major.

Yet.

Just enough to divert her, enough to stop Tessa giving an answer she would surely only live to regret.

'Max.' Ryan was bearing down on them, his face serious. 'We've got a problem.'

'Why's it always ''we'' when there's a problem?' Max said, a quick light joke before his face grew serious. 'What is it'

'Two kids out walking along the cliff at Burney's point. One of them lost his footing.'

'Go on.' He prompted.

'Apparently he's fallen onto a ledge, seemingly unconscious.' Ryan was talking as he ran back to the ambulance and Max and Tessa followed, Tessa urgently beckoning Jane to join her. 'The other kids made it back to get help, but the tide's coming in.'

Tessa pulled out the emergency cupboard keys from her pocket and unlocked the door by the ambulance bay as she took in the information as Max listened to the unfolding story.

'The chopper can't go out, the wind is too strong.'

'Who's with him at the moment?' Max asked urgently. 'I can give some instructions over the radio…'

'That's just it.' Ryan's face was lined with concern and the hairs on Tessa's neck stood up as his grim words reached her ears. 'No one's with him. We're the nearest crew. The rest are stuck with the traffic accident—we're going out to him now.'

He didn't ask if they could come, he didn't need to.

Tessa was in charge and technically should stay but, given Jane's neck and Kim's pregnancy, they weren't exactly inundated with options as to who should go out on the rescue.

Pulling off her shoes and top, Tessa didn't even feel a hint of embarrassment as she flashed rather too much creamy bust encased in a violet bra to her colleagues. They'd all seen worse.

'Jane, let the supervisor know—she's already sending two staff down. She'll come and oversee the department while I'm out.'

Jane nodded, or at least as much as she could with her wry neck.

In no time Tessa had pulled on her waterproof jacket and boots, and the paramedics helped her quickly load on her rucksack. Max, who had stripped off practically in the corridor, was already in the ambulance, flicking on the sirens to clear the road.

'Come on, guys,' he ordered as they piled in, Tessa pulling on a large red hard hat. She handed one of the same to Max who took it with barely a word of thanks, his mind already with his patient.

''Struth.' Ryan grinned, pulling out of the ambulance bay at breakneck speed. 'You wouldn't want to be married to him, Tessa. No chance of an extra coat of lipstick with him waiting in the driveway.'

At least Max had the grace to blush.

The roads *were* like glass, and even Max, who was straining at the bit to get there, didn't moan when Ryan took the bends relatively slowly. Another accident was the last thing they needed right now.

'How old?' Tessa asked.

'Around eleven—that's basically all we've got. He's fallen about ten metres, landed on a ledge halfway down Burney's lookout. Have you been there?'

Tessa shook her head but no one noticed. They were all shouting about the sirens. 'Too near the edge for me.'

'What time's the tide due in?' Max asked, looking down at his heavy watch and fiddling with what seemed an inordinate number of dials.

'Five-o-nine,' Ryan shouted, and Tessa, who had no more need for a sports watch than a size-eight dress, felt a little left out as Jim and Max programmed the contraptions on their wrists, her battered but much-loved fob watch obviously superseded.

'We've got back-up coming,' Jim shouted, relaying the crackling messages on the two-way radio, 'but they're well behind us. Most of the ambulances are with the RTA and a couple of fire trucks are coming from a nursing home.'

'There's a fire in a nursing home?' Tessa was aghast, frantically imagining the scene at Emergency if a home full of geriatrics suddenly started descending on them.

'The roof blew off, love.' Jim grinned. 'They'll be needing an extra mug of cocoa tonight.'

Burney's lookout was a small picnic area at the end of a long sandy track. The ambulance bumped along, its wheels swerving erratically in the soft, wet conditions, intermittently whirring as the vehicle threatened to get bogged down. 'We'll have to leave it here.'

As soon as the back of the ambulance opened, the full atrocity of the conditions hit Tessa. Rain lashed her face and the wind whipped her dark hair over her eyes, literally knocking the breath out of her. Running was a near impossible feat and she struggled with the weight of her backpack as the wind pushed her backwards.

'I can see him!' Ryan was lying on the small-decked area, his large frame a solid re-assuring figure, his words almost drowned out by the raging storm.

'Rope,' Max said, unceremoniously lash-ing a safety rope first around Tessa and then himself, securing them to the rather fragile-looking wooden fence. And for once Tessa didn't even think about holding her stomach in, her concern solely for the little boy, lying metres down on a ledge.

'He's moving.' Max was lying prostate next to Ryan, craning his neck for a better view, making futile attempts to call to the boy. His words were lost the second they left his lips. 'His legs are broken, but I definitely saw movement in his arm. I'm going down.'

'Hold on a sec, Doc.' Ryan shook his head. 'We need to assess things first.'

'What's to assess?' Max snapped. 'He's not going to walk up himself—look at his legs. And he's in no state to strap on a harness.'

'There's no trees nearby for one thing, so there's nothing stable to secure a rope to,' Ryan said, not remotely fazed by Max's agitation, too used to drama to risk a team with a hasty decision. 'And this fence isn't going to hold anything for long. We need to wait for back-up.'

'We could use the ambulance.' Max said urgently. 'That will hold us.'

But Ryan shook his head. 'That's what I was trying before—we can't get it in close enough.' Max was the doctor, theoretically in charge, but Ryan was a paramedic, used to rescue situations, used to battling appalling conditions, and Max respected that. 'If anyone goes down now, it will have to be you,' Ryan said to a nodding Max. 'Jim and I are too heavy for you lot to pull up, especially with a kid.' His words were delivered so calmly, so steadily that for a second Tessa relaxed. Ryan had it all under control, he was used to this type of emergency.

But just as Tessa felt her heart rate steady somewhat, felt the situation was coming under control, every last piece of order was shredded as a huge angry wave rolled in, its surf cascading over the edge, literally knocking Tessa from her feet. Such was its force Tessa was sure she would be swept away, the wooden boards slipping under her fingers as she fought to grab on, her boots slipping, offering no grip. She was sure the rope that the fence that was holding them would give way at any second.

A strong hand was holding her then, pulling her to her feet as the surf dashed angrily back, a tiny pause to gain their collective breaths as Max held her tight.

'You all right?'

Tessa could only nod, real fear clutching her now. She chewed her lip with nerves as Ryan lay back down, peering into the swirling froth of surf.

'He's still there,' Ryan shouted. 'The ledge is acting as a buffer.'

'For how long, though? Ryan, we've got to go down *now*!' Max was pulling on a harness, and Jim helped him secure it as Ryan pulled himself up. Tessa pulled the hard metal stretcher over but Ryan shook his head.

'There's no time for that. Just put the second harness on him and a hard collar if there's time, then I'm pulling you up. If that tide comes up any higher or you can't free him, I'm pulling you up anyway—got it?'

Max nodded, his face pale against the red hard hat, his mouth clamped firmly shut as Ryan shouted his orders over the wind.

'Come up backwards and keep your rucksack on—it will act as a shield against the cliff. Just wrap your arms around the kid and we'll haul you up.' He was checking the clips, pulling the straps tight. 'Tessa, you lie down and watch him. Jim and I are going to take the strain. You shout the orders and shout them loud.' One final quick check and

Ryan nodded his consent that it was time to move. 'It's going to hurt, mate.'

'Be careful.' Her teeth were chattering, her fear palpable. As Max leant back, took the first tentative step off the edge, tears coursed unnoticed down her cheeks. How she wanted to call him back, tell him it was too much to risk, too dangerous, but she knew deep down it would be useless. Max was going and there wasn't a single thing she could do.

The child wasn't moving now, his body lying awkwardly like a limp rag doll, his legs horribly distorted. But more alarming, from her precarious position Tessa could see the rise of the tide—even the smaller waves were dangerously lapping over the edge of the ledge, each breaking wave threatening to engulf the boy, to carry him out to the clutches of the ocean, away from any hope of survival.

Max was working his way down, his haste to get there tempered by the slippery rock and the engulfing wind and rain that made each movement a feat in itself. Shale was falling down the face of the cliff, each step resulting in a cascade of rock crashing into the ocean below.

'Wait!' Tessa's shout was urgent. The rope, the one thread of safety, was causing problems of it own, loosening the softened edges. She watched as Max paused, a storm of shale littering his helmet, his head lowering as it battered him, his arms too occupied with clinging on to act as a shield. Tessa watched helplessly as the hat, his only protection, slipped off, swirling as it fell into the murky depths, bobbing up and down in the angry surf.

'Max is bleeding,' Tessa shouted. 'He's lost his hat.'

'Pull him up.'

Tessa signalled their decision, but Max couldn't see her as his eyes were filled with blood, but as he felt the haul of the rope Tessa ignored Max's frantically shaking head, watching with a mixture of dread and relief as the paramedics hauled him up the cliff face, sensing his reluctance yet knowing there had been no choice.

No choice at all.

'I was nearly there,' Max yelled, almost sobbing with frustration as he lay muddied and breathless, thumping his fist into the ground as Ryan pulled off the harness.

'You've got a head wound.' Ryan was pushing a large wad against his forehead which was immediately soaked with the red of Max's blood.

'Bandage it up, let me have another go. I was almost there!' But his words were futile and everyone knew it. The rain and blood would render the bandage useless in seconds, and Max's face wasn't pale now, it was chalky white with a grey tinge around his lips as he battled with nausea and throbbing pain.

'We'll just have to wait for back-up.' Ryan's voice was sombre. 'It won't be much longer.' How hollow his words sounded, when all present knew that time wasn't on their side. Max's effort had been their one and only chance.

Unless…

'I'll go.' Tessa's words were delivered through chattering teeth, but her eyes were serious.

'Don't be ridiculous—' Max started, but Ryan looked up from the bandage he was applying and Tessa nodded, confirming her decision.

'I'm going down.'

CHAPTER SEVEN

TESSA wasn't heroic.

Heroic people rushed in with no thought for themselves, no doubt or wavering.

Tessa wavered.

'No way.' Max was struggling to stand. 'No way!' he yelled.

'I'm on a rope,' Tessa was shouting as Ryan strapped her in. 'They'll pull me up.' They would, too. Ryan and Jim would never let her fall—she knew that. This wasn't a foolhardy, futile attempt, or she wouldn't have volunteered.

But Max was having none of it. 'I'm in charge here.'

'Since when did you pull rank?' Tessa was shouting. 'I've trained for this! You went down, Max. Why's it so different for me?'

Her question went unanswered. She saw the defeat in his face as he watched her step back. It reminded her of relatives left in the interview room, utter helplessness mixed with fear. She knew that feeling—after all, the same panic had engulfed her when Max had gone down.

What goes up must come down. Or was it what goes down must come up?

Tessa had always thought her life would flash before her eyes, a horrible slow-motion version of all the mistakes she had made, all the ghastly first dates, the fashion *faux pas*, the first kiss that had ended in tears, rowing with her mum, kissing Max…

Unfortunately nothing so inviting gripped her as Tessa made the achingly treacherous journey down the cliff face. Instead, she struggled to remember a basic law of physics.

And if necessary, rewrite it. Tessa was definitely coming up!

Don't look down. Don't look down.

She chanted it in her mind, focussing only on her feet as she leant back into the harness, her legs like lead, the adrenaline pumping through her veins no match against the harsh elements, her wringing-wet clothes, her already fatigued muscles. Slowly, slowly Tessa inched her way down the cliff, slipping every now and then but righting herself. She *was* trained for this. Trips out with the chopper had been followed up with lectures and practicals, but plastic walls were no match for reality. Practice harness's in safe warm gyms nothing like the damp cold leather that cut into her thighs, the rope cutting into her hands, the spray of the surf forcing the breath out of her lungs. But there was an end in sight, the ledge inching closer, looming towards her with surprising speed, the feel of relatively solid ground so welcome that for an instant Tessa closed her eyes in relief.

Only for an instant.

He was breathing. That was the first thought that registered as the small boy came into her focus and Tessa crawled towards him.

Unconscious—that was her second thought.

The ledge that had protected him and saved him from the clutches of the ocean was protecting Tessa now, too. A jagged elevation providing a wave break, giving her room to work. Grappling at the equipment on her belt, she freed the cervical collar, but she could feel the tug of the rope on her waist and looking up, she saw Max frantically beckoning to warn her he was going to pull her up.

The collar was vital but, Tessa registered, useless if it meant she couldn't get him up and, forgoing the usual basic first-aid procedure, Tessa fumbled with the harness, clipping it into place with numb, frozen fingers. Pulling the innate body against her, she strapped him in just as she felt the rope grow taut.

One winch and she saw the reason behind Max's decision. The tide had risen even further; lapping around the ledge now, filling the small area she had only just left.

Two winches into the lift she remembered Ryan's ominous warning.

It's going to hurt, mate.

It hurt like hell. Buffeted against the rock, Tessa felt every jagged bump as she shielded the limp body as best she could. There had been no time for assessment, no time for anything. The spray was stinging now, filling her nostrils, making each breath painful, but an air of calmness was over her now she knew she was safe, knew she was nearly there.

But as relieved as she was, as blissfully grateful as Tessa felt, as solid arms pulled her up, she was feminine enough to feel a tinge of indignity as Ryan hauled her harness up over the edge, giving any passing ships and undoubted glimpse of her violet underwear.

Not that anyone noticed.

Lying stranded on the beautiful ground, Tessa struggled to catch her breath, coughing in violent, painful spasms. With salt water filling her nose, her eyes, her mouth, it was all she could do to lie there as they hastily unstrapped her patient from the harness, rushing him off to the relative safety of the ambulance, to the shiny equipment and oxygen cylinders he so desperately needed.

Tessa hadn't expected a fanfare, pats on the back or rounds of applause when she'd surfaced. She'd known that the patient had to take priority, but some recognition of her efforts wouldn't have hurt. It was slightly deflating to have to trudge back to the ambulance in the biting rain. Slipping in practically unnoticed, she sat on the seat, watching as they worked on the innate body of their patient.

Her patient.

'How's he doing?'

Her question went unanswered for a full twenty seconds as Max intubated him, slipping a plastic tube into his airway, then taping it securely in place. She felt him relax. With the airway secure, he could now deal with Tessa.

'Wrap a blanket around yourself,' Max shot at her without looking up.

Something in his voice told Tessa not to argue. Pulling the scratchy white blanket with fingers that wouldn't obey, the numbness was replaced by pain as her circulation returned with a vengeance. A bandage had been hastily tied around Max's head—very hastily, it would appear! It looked more like a bandanna, and his left eye was already starting to close over.

'How is he, Max?' Tessa heard more than felt her teeth chattering violently. Desperately she struggled to keep her voice normal, to belie the dizziness, the nausea that was starting to engulf her, the full realisation of what had taken place only just starting to surface.

'We need to get him to the hospital. What's the ETA, Ryan?'

'Fifteen minutes if we step on it.'

'Put your foot down and make it ten,' Max said tersely, his obvious desire to get there confirming the precariousness of the child's situation. 'Let the hospital know. Near drowning, multiple fractures, head injury. Tell them to have the paediatrician and ortho waiting…' His eyes caught Tessa's and she waited, for what she didn't know.

A half-smile, a nod of appreciation, some acknowledgment at least, but the anger blazing from his eyes floored even Tessa for a moment.

'You'd have done the same, Max,' Tessa argued, without obvious provocation, his angry silence speaking volumes.

'You ignored a direct order,' Max retorted, refusing to give an inch.

'Oh, and you're such a stickler for the rules.'

Max was staring at the monitor now, his finger resting on the child's neck, gently assessing the child's body, but still Tessa braced herself. Max could do ten things at once, and delivering a short sharp lecture wouldn't break his concentration for a second.

'I got him up, didn't I?' Tessa argued to her unresponsive audience. Jim gave an apologetic shrug, refusing to get involved. 'And with no harm done. I'm fine.'

'You're fine.' Lifting his arm, Max gripped the flask of Haemaecel and squeezed it hard. 'Run through the blood, Jim—this kid needs it.'

'You're fine?' he repeated. Two conversations were going on at once and Tessa knew from the angry shift in his voice that she was the recipient of the last two words. 'You could have been killed down there, you're covered in bruises and you've swallowed half the ocean, but at least you're ''fine.'''

'How dare you?' Despite her chattering teeth, Tessa managed to put some force into her voice, her words coming out in a strange staccato. 'How dare you have a go at me for doing exactly the same as you? I was doing my job, Max. I'm trained for this.'

'Ten minutes in a gym does not constitute—' He was in full swing now. Connecting the blood, Max stood up, holding the bag high so the precious liquid flowed more quickly into the pale limp body, one white tense hand holding the rack above him as the ambulance hurtled through the streets.

'Max, please, stop...'

'I will not stop. If I wanted to, I could write an incident report. If I wanted to, I could make sure you never go out on another rescue. There's a pecking order for a reason, Tessa. There's a leader because someone has to make the calls, make the decisions, and today it was me and you deliberately, blatantly defied me.'

'Please, Max…' His harsh words were possibly merited, Tessa conceded, and any other time she could have dealt with them, argued her point, bit back with a smart reply or a persuasive argument, but a black wave of nausea, more overwhelming than the waves she had so recently faced, was rolling in now, overwhelming her with ten times the force of the ocean as the ambulance floor spun like a merry-go-round at the fairground. 'Stop.'

'No, I will not stop. Just because you've done the trauma course,' Max ranted, his eyes on the patient, completely missing the grey tinge to her lips, the beads of sweat forming on her brow.

'Max…' Tessa lurched as he finally turned his head and saw her. 'I'm going to be sick.'

There was nothing she could do to take away the indignity of the situation. Max, one hand on the IV flask, none too gently pushed her head between her knees with the other as Jim handed her a plastic bag and Tessa hunched over it, crying, retching and utterly, completely humiliated as Max was yet again proved right.

She must have swallowed half the ocean.

She was too weak, too exhausted to offer any assistance as the ambulance screeched into the hospital grounds. In seconds the stretcher was being rushed though to Resus and all Tessa could do was sit in the back, white and shaking, until Kim appeared some moments later.

'Max told me to come and fetch the heroine.'

'Max said no such thing,' Tessa said ruefully, managing a very weak grin. 'Hit me with the truth. What did he really say?'

'OK, he told me to make sure ''the idiot who risked her neck'' got into some warm clothes and had her bruises checked over.'

'I don't need to be checked over,' Tessa said, taking Kim's arms and somewhat unsteadily stepping out of the ambulance, her legs trembling violently. 'But, yes, please to the warm clothes. How's the child? Have we got a name yet?'

'Jamie Hunter, and he's not eleven—he's a small thirteen and according to his friend drank the best part of a bottle of wine. Probably why he's still alive, he must have bounced all the way down.'

'Great.'

The last thing Tessa wanted was to be checked over, particularly as a very unruffled Emily breezed into the cubicle.

'Look at you,' she said, her blue eyes wide. 'You look as if you've been dragged through a hedge backwards.'

'Dragged up a cliff actually. Look, Emily, I'm fine, just a few bruises.'

'You know you need to be seen. Jamie's in X-ray. He's got more than enough staff with him so Max asked if I could look you over as I'm the only female doctor down here.'

Max probably thought he was being sensitive, Tessa thundered internally as she stripped off her clothes and pulled on a gown then lay down on the hard trolley and awaited inspection. Emily might be the only female doctor on, but she was also size eight, honey brown and had probably only ever seen cellulite on one of her patients.

Well, she was about to get an eyeful now!

'My goodness.' Emily hastily sketched a rather unflattering body on the casualty card and proceeded to document Tessa's multiple bruises. 'You're going to be sore.'

'I already am,' Tessa muttered as nimble fingers probed her, not even bothering to pull in her stomach as Emily pushed and prodded. What was the point?

There was no competition.

Even Emily's nails were gorgeous. Tessa sighed to herself, blushing to her roots at the indignity of it all. Not flash and long, just very white and very neat, her diamond ring flashing now and then as it caught one of the overhead lights.

'Nothing broken,' Emily concluded. 'No signs of concussion.'

'Can I get back to work, then?'

'The only place you're going,' Emily said firmly, 'is bed. I'll give you a choice, though. You can either go home without argument, or I'll admit you to the obs ward.'

'I'm supposed to be taking Jane home,' Tessa protested, but even that was thwarted as a concerned-looking Jane bobbed into the cubicle.

'Take your own advice, Tessa—get a cab charge. The staff car park's going to be full tonight with Emergency staff's cars. Max won't be driving with that gash on his head. He needs stitches,' Jane added. 'Chris is going to do it.'

'No way,' Emily said, a very tight smile appearing at edge of her lips. 'That pleasure will be entirely mine.' Signing off the casualty card, she turned her blue eyes on Tessa. 'Home or the obs ward?'

'Home,' Tessa grumbled, lying back resignedly against the white pillow.

'I'll give you a note till Monday. Just one other thing...' The fun hadn't quite finished, though, and Emily gave a small apologetic smile as Tessa waited for the inevitable question, rolling up the sleeve of her hospital gown with a miserable sigh before the words had even left Emily's lips. 'When did you last have a tetanus shot?'

Only when she was gone did Tessa sit up. 'I'll be in tomorrow, so don't go booking any staff.'

'She's given you four days off,' Jane argued. 'Take it, I know I would.'

'I'm just bruised. I'll see how I feel tomorrow. Anyway, I've got Max's present to bring in. He'll have to have it in the bag, there's no way I'm stopping at the milk bar for wrapping paper looking like this!'

Shooing everyone out, Tessa pulled on some clean, dry theatre blues. She didn't want to go home, she wanted to see how Jamie was doing, wanted to be *in there* working on him, following her patient through. And later, when he had been moved to the ward or transferred, she wanted to sit down with her colleagues and a steaming mug of coffee to talk things out, to go over and over their movements, their decisions, to debate the whys and wherefores, to prophesy on the outcomes.

Sure, no doubt on Monday a memo would appear in her pigeonhole, inviting her to talk things through in a cosy little 'chat' with the staff counsellor, but formal debriefing had never done it for Tessa. There was something so clinical, so wooden about sitting on a hard-backed chair with a salaried face nodding you on, urging you to reveal all, to *share* how it had been for you as you'd dangled off a cliff face, pulled a child from the clutches of the ocean. What would they know about the impulse, the passion, the dedication that spurred Emergency workers on, made them walk that extra mile for someone they had never even met? How could they understand her motives behind ringing up later tonight, the dread as you waited to be connected, the relief if he was still hanging in there, the utter despair if it had all been futile. How could her feelings be summed up in a paragraph in her staff file?

Coffee and the staffroom did it for Tessa every time.

Tessa saw Max briefly as she made her way to the ambulance bay. He was wheeling his patient back from X-ray and by the grim look on his face Tessa knew she hadn't been forgiven.

'Are you going home?' He nodded to the staff to go on without him.

'Apparently so.' Tessa shrugged. 'I wasn't exactly given a say in the matter.'

'Did someone check you over?'

'Your fiancée.' Tessa bit back, smiling sweetly, though it stopped far short of her eyes. 'How's Jamie?'

'He's got multiple leg fractures, but you knew that anyway. Thankfully his neck looks OK on the films and the CT scan of his abdomen came up clear.'

'What about his head injury?'

'Hard to say.' Max was looking at the floor, the walls, anywhere but at Tessa. 'Once the alcohol wears off we'll be better able to assess his neurological status. Tessa, back there at Burney's—'

'You were out of line, Max,' Tessa finished for him.

'No, Tessa, I wasn't. I was in charge, it was my call as to who went down there.'

'Someone had to.'

'No, they didn't. Someone has to make the calls, and in my opinion it was just too dangerous. The tide was practically in, the cliff face was unstable and we had no back-up. You put yourself at risk, at serious risk, and before you snap back that I did the same, I'm more experienced, I've done abseiling—'

'Yes, sir.'

'What's that supposed to mean?' Max barked.

'I feel like a schoolgirl getting a telling-off. I'm nearly thirty, Max, I've got a nursing degree, I've done my advance trauma course and I've been out on plenty rescues. Admittedly, I don't spend my days off dangling off cliff faces in the name of pleasure and I'm not an expert on walking boots or the benefits of reef knots as opposed to...' Tessa searched her mind for another example, but her time in the Guides was a very distant memory. 'To other types of knots,' Tessa finished lamely.

A tiny smile was starting to tug at the corner of his lips, so tiny it was barely there.

'But I wasn't on a suicide mission out there, Max. I wouldn't have gone down if I genuinely didn't think I was capable. Now, if you've quiet finished lecturing me, my taxi's here, I'd like to get home,' Tessa lied, haughtily pulling her bag over her shoulder, then immediately regretting it. There was obviously a bruise there that Emily had missed.

'Will you be OK?'

'I'm off duty, Max.' Tessa shrugged. 'So it's not your concern.'

Walking out to the ambulance bay, Tessa didn't look back, didn't even bother to say goodbye.

There would be plenty of time for all that tomorrow.

CHAPTER EIGHT

NEVER had a warm bubble bath been so gratefully received. Wincing as she lowered herself, Tessa lay for ages, topping up the water every now and then, staring at the ceiling, torturing herself by going over and over recent events—the inquest, the kiss, the moment of weakness before the call-out.

The rescue didn't even get a look in.

Pulling out the plug, Tessa rubbed moisturiser into every inch of her bruised, battered body, then ran a brush listlessly through her hair before padding into her bedroom.

So much for wowing Max at his leaving party, Tessa thought, looking at the grey strappy dress she had bought on her most recent spending spree. Not that wowing Max had ever been on the agenda, but she would at least have liked to have looked good when she said goodbye, let him glimpse what he was missing.

There was no chance of that now, no hope of wowing anyone. The only thing in her room that would cover all her bruises was the sunflower bedspread and a pair of gumboots!

The next time I fall in love, Tessa thought crossly, lying on the bed and staring at yet another ceiling, it will be with a nice uncomplicated single man, who absolutely adores me, and perhaps most importantly has never even set foot inside a hospital.

Doctors with over-inflated egos were way down on her list of priorities!

Next time.

Exploring her wounded heart, Tessa felt a tiny spark of hope. There would be a next time. Just because she had been hurt, it didn't mean there wasn't someone out there for her. Someone who would love her, adore her and, more importantly, someone who was free to love her.

It wasn't as if she was short of offers. OK, she didn't have traffic-stopping good looks or a figure to die for, but the only person who seemed to mind about her weight was Tessa herself, and what man would ever complain that her breasts were too large?

There was a world of opportunity out there, but just as surely as hope sparked it faded. The one image she couldn't shake, the one person she truly loved coming into her focus, drowning out all other images.

Max.

It wasn't a man she wanted, a boyfriend, a partner for the sake of it. She wasn't lonely or dissatisfied with life; there wasn't an aching gap that could only be filled by a male presence.

It was all about Max.

All of it.

Normally Tessa wouldn't have answered the door wrapped in a towel, but when the doorbell rang out, there was nothing normal about the way Tessa was feeling. So fed up was Tessa that for once in her life she was determined to hastily bid the inevitable salesman goodbye without receiving a ten-minute sales pitch, or give a polite 'Not interested' to religious converters instead of ending up the recipient of a pile of brochures and the promise of a follow-up visit.

The only trouble was, her list of possibilities hadn't included Max Slater, standing on her step, bruised and gorgeous, and Max didn't need to deliver a sales pitch, she'd already sampled the goods. And as for converting her...

'Thought you could use this.' He held up a bottle of brandy, looking unsure of his reception, as if any second he might change his mind and bolt back down her rather overgrown garden path.

'I don't like brandy.' It wasn't the wittiest answer, but it beat slamming the door in his face, which was her second reaction.

Pulling him in and burying her face in Max's chest had been Tessa's first.

'Strictly for medicinal purposes.'

Only her head was peering around the door and she eyed him suspiciously.

'How's Jamie?'

'Good.' Max shrugged. 'Well, that's a slight exaggeration. He's better than I thought he would be. We were about to transfer him to an intensive care bed at the children's hospital but he started fighting the tube and we extubated him. He's on a high-dependency bed on the children's ward.'

'Do you think he'll have brain damage?'

'If he hasn't now, he will once his father gets hold of him.' The tiny joke relaxed her and her hand, which had been gripping the door so tightly, relaxed as she laughed.

Big mistake.

As the door swung open slightly his eyes drifted down over her body, his unsure look instantly replaced by horror, but thankfully, having seen herself in the bedroom mirror, Tessa knew that it wasn't her rather generously proportioned body having that negative effect on him.

'It's not as bad as it looks,' she said almost defensively.

'It looks terrible.' Max walked into her home uninvited, but shamefully welcome, and it felt so strange to be standing before him, scantily dressed on the threshold of something far more treacherous than a cliff face in a storm.

There was no safety harness here, no manuals dictating procedures, no leaders, only followers.

And following your heart was a dangerous, dangerous game.

'Oh, Tessa.' His hands gently explored the purple angry swelling on her shoulder and she winced involuntarily at his touch, her head telling herself to stop this now, while every shredded nerve end seemed to scream internally for more. For his cool fingers to soothe, for his gentle touch to massage away the pain. 'I'm sorry I shouted. You were right to go down, I know that. I've just never been so scared...' Troubled eyes looked up and found hers. 'Actually, that's not true.'

'Isn't it?' Even her voice sounded strange, as if it belonged to someone else. The Tessa she knew, the Tessa whose body she'd lived in for the last twenty-nine years, would have stopped this before it had even started, never let him in the door dressed only in a towel, would have demanded answers, explanations, but right now all Tessa could live for was this moment.

'Leaving you behind, Tessa, that's what scares me the most.'

'Emily...'

'It's over, Tessa, I promise you. I can't explain it yet. Surely you know by now that I'd never hurt you. That you can trust me.'

And despite it all, despite the unanswered questions, she did trust him. Max was her safety harness, the one waiting at the top, Max who would never, ever let her fall. Max, who despite his vocal reservations had given her the strength to go down. And it was Max now who was giving her the strength to go on, to cast aside her doubts, to take the whole thing to its natural inevitable conclusion. All she wanted, needed, desired was now.

Tessa trusted him, and for now at least, that was enough. Saturated with emotion, trembling at his presence, the horrible, horrible days that had preceded this moment seemed to melt away, and all Tessa wanted was the feel of his lips on hers, for the bliss of his touch on the one part of her body that wasn't aching or sore or utterly, completely devastated.

She wanted him to kiss it better, to take away the doubt and the pain and swear it wouldn't come back in the morning. And when his lips met hers, when they moved in heated unison, when his arms gently wrapped around hers, this time she didn't push him away, it was Tessa that pulled him closer. And later, when kissing wasn't enough to quell their desires, when his gentle, wary touch wasn't sufficient to stem the rising tide, when his whispered words were no longer what she needed to hear, it was Tessa who finally followed her heart and led him to the bedroom, Tessa who held her breath in wonder as he impatiently pulled off his clothes. She stared at him for a moment. Five years of imagining, five years of longing and still her mind hadn't done him justice. She had thought him thin, but the man standing naked before her was toned and as muscular as an athlete. His chest bore the bruises of the rescue, purple bruises beneath the soft mat of hair that dusted his chest, silken not wiry, she registered as her trembling hand brushed over it, his nipples mahogany, down, ever down her fingers worked, boldly taking him in her hands, touching him tentatively, her eyes wide in excited wonder at the bliss of feeling him, swollen and warm in her gently cupped hand. Looking up for a moment, she was almost knocked sideways by the lust in his eyes, the boyish, mischievous face she had known so well lost now for ever as he smiled the intimate smile of a lover.

'Seems you are an expert on knots after all.' Somehow her towel had stayed up and Max's impatient fingers wrestled with the tie. One small final joke, one last glimpse at her friend before he became her lover. As the towel slipped down to the floor, as Tessa stood there she waited, wishing she'd kept to one of her thousand diets, wishing her battered body wasn't how he'd see her for the first time. But any doubts she'd had, any niggling feelings of insecurity were dispelled in an instant when she saw the wonder in his eyes, felt the passion in his touch as with a low moan he buried his face in her splendid bosom, his lips brushing the white creamy flesh, his tongue working its magic on her jutting pink nipples as his hand slipped between her parted thighs, her groin lifting toward him like a reflex action, small gasps coming from her throat as his mere touch had her pulsing, writhing in the palm of his hand.

She felt beautiful, voluptuous, gorgeous, his reverence, his sheer delight in her body utterly empowering her. Never had she felt more feminine, more graceful, more proud. The bed was only a metre away but he picked her up with ease and laid her down tenderly before bringing his body over her, loving her with his eyes as he explored her with his hands, parting her legs with his own he rocked back on his heels and she lay there writhing with lust, her pelvis jutting impatiently, silently begging him to enter her.

But Max had waited for this moment too long to rush things. Slowly he held the peach of her buttocks, explored her with his tongue, his eyes occasionally looking up, capturing every image of her gasping, shuddering climax, and when the last flickers of her climax had abated, when she was sure she could never feel that way again and live to tell the tale, Max stoked the fires of her passion again, filling her with his manhood this time, pushing her to the absolute limits of endurance, delving ever deeper into her as she bucked against him, driving him on, urging him still deeper, her legs coiling around his back, calves gripping his waist. He could never be too close, his body never too near. Five years of hidden passion, buried desire and burning desperate need were expended with the explosion of their union. So sweet the passion, the pain of before was dispelled in that instant, the questions that had tormented her forgotten now as she lay, breathless, exhausted but utterly adored in the arms of her lover, their bodies wrapped together, and for the first time in half a decade Tessa slept as nature intended: with Max by her side.

CHAPTER NINE

GINGERLY Tessa felt her head, her fingers probing her scalp, praying to find a bump, a tender spot that she could possibly blame her moment's madness on.

Nothing.

Turning, her eyes drifted over Max who slumbered on, a half-smile on his face, his eye swollen and black, his body a swirling mass of bruises, hair tousled and unkempt, a dark shadow smudging his chin.

Never had he looked more beautiful.

Slowly Tessa inched herself out of bed. There wasn't much choice *but* to move slowly, her body felt as it had the morning after her first and final aerobics class. Every muscle seemed an inch shorter, every movement stiff and unnatural. Padding down the hall, she eyed the untouched brandy bottle ruefully.

She couldn't even blame it on alcohol—they hadn't had a drop.

The shower helped somewhat, a whole tank of hot water, and gradually her body started to relax, to move a bit more freely. Aiming the dwindling hot water on her neck, Tessa rotated her head, trying and failing not to think of Max lying just a matter of feet away in *her* bed.

They had made love, blissful wonderful love. She had succumbed without question, without even a hint of resistance, accepted without argument that she could trust him, that it was over with Emily.

But was it?

I'd never hurt you. Max's words echoed through her mind.

You can trust me.

The water was running cold now but Tessa barely noticed. She wanted so badly to trust him, to believe what he had said, but what had seemed so straightforward last night suddenly appeared terribly complicated.

He was flying to England tomorrow.

How could she not be hurt?

The questions rattled on unanswered as Tessa waited for the kettle to boil and, gazing at the rising steam, she debated how to play this. Should she confront him now, ask him to come into the kitchen away from the warm bed and inevitable temptations, or wake him with a kiss and a coffee, slip between the sheets and let Max hold her, listen to his story, let him explain how they were going to play things? How they were going to tell everyone that they were now a couple...

It wasn't going to be easy, Tessa knew that, but as she poured the water into the cups, a smile played on her lips. With Max beside her she could face anything. It was a delicious problem: they were in love, it was over with Emily, they'd done nothing wrong.

If only she could have captured that moment, held onto that feeling for just a moment longer, but as she pulled the milk carton out of the fridge and the telephone rang, she answered it with such a smile in her voice, but every tiny fledgling dream she was nurturing wilted as the crisp, businesslike voice of Emily winged its way down the telephone into her kitchen and into reality.

'Tessa, sorry to ring you at home.'

'That's fine, no problem.'

'Are you still thinking of coming in?'

She was tempted to say no, to slam down the telephone and dive under the quilt in her bedroom, but Tessa knew deep down that would solve nothing. Her bemusement with Emily ringing her for a moment overrode her nervousness. 'I'm just getting ready, actually.' Tessa hesitated, her cheeks burning, anticipating confrontation. Surely the guilt she was feeling was misplaced? Surely? 'What's the problem?'

'It's Kim.'

Tessa initial relief that it was obviously a work call was instantly replaced by guilt and concern as Emily continued.

'She's just been brought in by ambulance, she's bleeding heavily.'

'Oh, no.' Tessa felt sick to her stomach, hating herself for the relief that had flooded

her, all thoughts of Max, Emily and the hope-
less triangle she had joined forgotten as she
thought of her friend and colleague and the
baby Kim so desperately wanted.

'Has she lost the baby?'

'We're not sure yet. Tessa, her husband's
away on business and Kim's come in to the
department by herself and she's terrified,
she's really not telling me much. She's bleeding quite heavily but apart from letting me
put in an IV she won't let me near her. She
doesn't want to hear the news if it's bad, I
think.'

'That would be it.' Tessa's mind raced.
'This is a very precious baby. They've had
years of IVF, and from what she'd told me
it's their last go.'

'Well, she's just mentioned to me that
she's spoken with you about it. Now, her
husband's in Perth so even if he jumps on the
next plane it's going to be lunchtime before
he gets here. I wondered if you could try talking to her—she's so scared, but a friendly
face might help. If she's lost the baby I think

she'll need to go to Theatre fairly soon so we can try to stop the bleeding. I've rung my father and he's coming in, but without an ultrasound there's not a lot anyone can do.'

'I'll come straight in.'

'Thanks, Tessa. Sorry to wake you.'

'No problem, I was up anyway.' She was about to ring off but, instantly regretting it as the words spilled out of her mouth, Tessa prolonged the conversation. 'How come you saw her, Emily? I didn't think miscarriages were the ortho's domain.'

'Oh, sorry.' Emily laughed. 'I didn't explain myself very well, did I? I covered Emergency last night—I finish up at nine. I'm supposed to be on call tonight and tomorrow, so I owe a lot of favours with people covering for me. But with Max going, I couldn't miss his party. Our families are getting together for a barbecue tomorrow before we all head off for the airport, so I don't suppose we'll exactly be having a romantic last few hours. Still, it's worth a try.'

Strange how Tessa's voice managed to stay calm, despite the strangled scream that resonated in her head; strange how she even managed a couple more minutes of chit-chat as her world caved in around her. As if on autopilot, Tessa added the milk to her cup and drank it quickly, staring out of her window at the ocean. How calm it looked now, how hard to believe that only yesterday it had been a treacherous black hellhole, and now the water looked as clear and still as glass.

She had believed Max, trusted him, loved him.

And now she was paying the price.

Walking into the bedroom, she stood for a moment or two gazing at him, as calm and unruffled as the ocean, belying the awful deceitful lies he had told her, everything she had wanted to hear just so he could get her into bed.

Tessa toyed for a second with ripping off the sheet, pulling the pillow from under him, screaming her accusations, demanding his answers, his pathetic attempts at an explanation—but what would that solve?

What could he possibly say?

She dressed quietly, slipping his leaving present into her bag and picking up her shoes so as not to wake him.

The last thing Tessa wanted now was a fight.

She couldn't change the past, couldn't take away what had happened last night, and though shame, guilt and anger swept through her, deep down neither did Tessa want to erase it. Last night had been the happiest night of her life. One tiny glimpse of paradise to sustain her.

Quiet tears slid down her cheeks as she stared at the man she had loved, the man she had trusted above all else. This was how she would remember him; this was the image she would try to hold onto.

Max lying warm and sweet in her bed.

Quietly pulling the front door closed, a devilish smile broke through her tear-streaked face.

So what if she hadn't set the alarm?

Let Max come up with an excuse for his lateness.

'Sorry, Tessa.' Kim's face crumpled as Tessa pulled back the curtain. 'You're supposed to be off sick.'

'Shh...' Tessa wrapped her arms around Kim's heaving shoulders. 'You've nothing to be sorry for. As if I'd leave you on your own at a time like this. I was coming in anyway.'

'I'm bleeding.'

Tessa nodded, but didn't say anything. With Kim in this friable emotional state it was important not to rush things, to let Kim's story unfold at its own pace.

'Mark can't get a flight until nine, but he'll be here by this afternoon.'

'That's good.' Tessa undid the side of the trolley and perched herself on the edge.

'I think I've lost the baby.'

A long silence filled the air and when Kim didn't elaborate Tessa tentatively spoke. 'How much are you bleeding?'

'A lot back at home.' Kim lay back on the pillow, her face almost as white as the cotton. 'It seems to have stopped now.'

'Do you have any pain?'

'None.' Kim's eyes looked up, suddenly hopeful. 'That's a good sign, isn't it?'

It was a good sign, but a large bleed was still ominous and the last thing Tessa wanted to do was raise false hope. 'It can be,' she said gently. 'But until we do an ultrasound it's really just guesswork.'

'I mean, we don't know that I've lost it, it's not as if Emily's examined me.'

Kim was starting to get upset again, her labile mood swinging between hope and despair, and Tessa moved quickly to stabilise her, refusing to be drawn into Kim's irrational yet utterly understandable mind games. 'She won't examine you yet,' Tessa said firmly, 'because *if* the baby is still there and your uterus is a bit irritated, an internal might exacerbate things. We really need to do an ultrasound.'

'Now?'

Tessa nodded as Kim took a deep breath.

'Will you stay?'

'Of course I will. Can I get Emily?'

It was Kim who nodded now, and Tessa popped her head out of the cubicle nodding to Emily who was waiting with the ultrasound machine.

'She's ready.'

Kim was ready, almost, but as the cold blue jelly was squeezed onto her softly rounded abdomen she stalled at the final hurdle.

'I shouldn't have told everyone,' she sobbed. 'People are going to think—'

'Kim.' Tessa's voice was firm but kind. 'One of the most stupid things I've heard of is not telling people until a woman is passed her first trimester.' She watched as Kim frowned, the tears stilling for a second. 'Why shouldn't people know what you're going through? Why would it hurt less if you lost your baby at eight weeks or fourteen? If it's a wanted baby it's going to be agony, and having your friends know the hell you're going through can only help. This baby has been your dream and if you do lose it you're going to need your friends around you more than ever. It isn't silly or stupid, and there's nothing wrong with a bit of sympathy.'

The words reached her and as Kim lay back to find out what fate had in store for her, Tessa looked up at Emily, expecting her to begin the procedure, expecting her calm, unruffled colleague to be patiently waiting to start. Nothing, but nothing prepared Tessa for the sight of Emily with tears coursing down her cheeks, her shaking hands fiddling with dials on the machine.

'I'm fine,' Emily mouthed, obviously not wanting her sudden distress acknowledged, putting up her hand to still Tessa whose first instinct had been to go over to her. The glint of her diamond ring shamed Tessa back on the trolley and such was her guilt, her utter despair, Tessa felt like crying herself.

'Let's find out, shall we?' Tessa said, her voice shaky with emotion as Emily wiped her face with a tissue and picked up the probe.

Nursing had its good points, its great points even. There was elation, satisfaction when things went well, but it was tempered all too often with moments of great sadness. Times when no matter what you did, no matter what you said, no matter what the technology or equipment available, it was rammed home that greater forces in the world operated. That life wasn't always kind or fair—sometimes it was downright cruel.

Gripping Kim's hand, Tessa awaited the inevitable, pushed her problems to one side in the name of professionalism and searched her mind for words that might, if not comfort Kim, make this horrible situation no worse than it already was.

Emily had turned down the volume on the ultrasound machine and the screen was turned away. Tessa watched Kim, tears still managing to slip out from her tightly shut eyes as Emily moved the probe backwards and forwards for what seemed an inordinate amount of time then fiddled some more with the controls.

A whooshing rhythmic sound suddenly filled the room and Tessa jumped almost as much as Kim.

'Normal heart rate.' Emily was smiling now and it was happy tears glistening in her bright blue eyes. 'You've got yourself a little fighter in there.'

'I'm still pregnant?' Kim gasped.

'Absolutely.' Emily turned the screen around and they all stared in wonder at the screen, the unmistakable image of a baby, little knees tucked up, five tiny fingers attached to a tiny hand, oblivious of the distress the anxiety it had created.

'But how?' Kim begged.

'I'll have to leave that question for Dr Elves to answer.' Emily smiled. 'He shouldn't be too much longer. He'll do a more thorough ultrasound. But from what I can see, the placenta is nice and high, and the baby's not in any distress. Sometimes bleeds just happen and we never really know why.'

'Could I still lose it?'

'Let's wait for Dr Elves, shall we?' Emily said gently. 'This is very positive news, but you know no one can give you a cast-iron guarantee. We'll just have to take it a day at a time.'

'Dr Elves?' Kim's eyebrows furrowed. 'You've both got the same name.'

Emily grinned. 'He's my father, and don't tell him I told you this but he's also a great doctor, he'll look after you.'

'Thanks, Emily.' Kim turned slightly. 'And thanks, Tessa—for coming in, I mean.'

'Don't even mention it. Now, you lie back and get some rest. Do you want me to bring the phone in so you can ring your husband? This might make his flight a bit more bearable.'

'Please.'

There was an awful awkward moment as they left the cubicle. Tessa was a kind person and normally without question she would have guided Emily to the coffee-room, or at the very least checked that she was OK, put a hand on her arm and asked how she was doing.

But how could she now?

How could she look her colleague in the eye and ask if everything was OK when Max was lying in her bed?

The weight of her guilt, her deception chilled her to the core, made the nausea of yesterday seem like a walk in the park by comparison.

'Sorry about before.' Emily gave a thin laugh. 'I've been up all night, you know how it is.'

'Sure.'

Maybe she should tell Emily, Tessa mused as she busied herself around the department. But clearing her own conscience wouldn't help anyone. It was up to Max to tell her, up to Max and Emily to sort out whatever mess they were in. But Tessa knew this much— Max could walk in now and tell Emily it was over in full view of the department, but it was too late.

She could never want him now. Tessa mentally kicked herself. Wrong, Tessa, you'll always want him but you're never going to have him, she corrected. He'd left it too late. How could she ever trust him now?

Every traffic jam he got stuck in, every shift that went on too long or night out with his friends would have her wondering if she was getting her just desserts.

If he was doing to her what he had done to Emily.

If that larrikin smile, those cheeky good looks and that silver tongue were working their way into some other unsuspecting heart.

'Have you seen Max?' Everyone seemed to be asking, everyone was checking their watches or looking up at the clock. Tessa's cheeks burnt ever darker as she fiddled with the roster and directed the traffic in the corridor.

Max Slater might flaunt the rules now and then but he was never late.

Never.

In between asking where Max was, everyone seemed to be humming 'Leaving on a Jet Plane' and even Tessa, who hadn't even known she knew a John Denver song, found herself idly humming it as she sat on hold as the nurse supervisor yet again tried to come up with a valid reason as to why they couldn't have an agency nurse for the night shift.

'There you are!'

Emily smiled as Max rushed in, still unshaven, pulling his stethoscope out of his pocket and wrapping it around his neck.

'Where have you been, Slater?' Chris asked good-naturedly. 'You haven't left us yet.'

'Sorry, guys.' He looked as flustered as Tessa felt and she mumbled into the telephone even though the piped music was still playing in her ear.

'I tried to ring you at six.' Emily nudged him as she brushed past. 'Where on earth were you?'

'I didn't hear it,' Max muttered. 'I'll explain later, Emily,' he added quietly.

You liar. The words were on the tip of Tessa's tongue and for the tiniest instant her angry eyes flashed up at him, his obvious guilt as he looked away twisting the knife already lodged in her heart one turn tighter, but her angry words were never spoken. Instead, they screamed through her mind as the nurse supervisor came back onto the line.

'Look, I know the staff want to go to Max's leaving party but the department still has to be covered internally. And as for tomorrow, do you have any idea what an agency nurse costs to cover a Saturday night?'

'Of course I do,' Tessa argued. 'I'm the one who tackles the roster every week, but this is a genuine shortfall that's not our fault. Kim had agreed to work the night shift this weekend, she's hardly capable now.'

'I'm sorry, Tessa, you'll just have to work something out.'

'Tessa.' Max caught her as she came off the telephone. 'Can we go somewhere to talk?'

'Here will have to do, Max.' She didn't snap, didn't even wither him with a look, but her voice told him her answer was non-negotiable. 'I'm busy.'

'You should have woken me.' He was trying not whisper, but from the nervous shift of his eyes as he checked the coast was clear, Tessa was in no doubt his words were definitely for her ears only. 'You know we need to talk, Tessa, and you know damn well that it's impossible to do that here.'

Tessa nodded. It was as much of an answer as he was going to get.

'Tonight,' Max begged. 'At my party, don't dash off.'

'What, you'll try and squeeze me in a five-minute time slot?'

'Don't judge me, Tessa,' he pleaded. 'Not without hearing me out first. Tonight, we'll talk tonight.'

Again she nodded, but her eyes stayed fixed on the floor.

'Over here, Max.' Chris's voice had that slightly urgent ring to it that meant time was of the essence and Max was left with no choice but to go. 'Tonight,' he said again as he dashed off. But even before he had left the tiny annexe, before the scent of him had cleared, Tessa had picked up the telephone.

'About those night shifts,' Tessa said slowly. 'I've just found someone to fill them.'

They had their own little party for Max at lunchtime. A quick call to the local pizza shop, a crate of cola and enough chips and dips to feed an army.

People came and went often in hospital life. Six-month contracts, two years sometimes, but inevitably people moved on to pastures new. To bigger, slicker hospitals or poorer developing countries. There was a world of pain out there and a bayside hospital in Victoria wasn't going to hold everyone for ever.

Not even Tessa.

Her notice was already written in her head.

Even dream jobs had their downsides.

But today wasn't about Tessa and how she was going to live with her guilt, it wasn't about Emily and the fact her fiancé was leaving, it wasn't even about the department and how it was going to cope.

It was about Max.

Dr Max Slater, who had given his all to his beloved department, who had pulled the staff up when they'd been down, created comradeship when there had been conflict and managed to put a smile on everyone's face over the years.

So they raised their plastic cups to wish him well, and listened as the speeches droned on, tucking into pizza with one ear on the intercom, ready to be called away at any given moment. And Tessa finally realised that Max was right to go.

He had a talent, a God-given talent that saved lives, a career that needed to be furthered. And when finally it was Tessa's turn she plastered on her usual smile and stood at the front of the staffroom and made the hardest speech of her life.

'I'm not going to inflate your ego further, Max, by telling you all how much we'll miss you.' She smiled hard, absolutely determined not to cry. 'I think you know that already. All I'm going to say is that we all wish you well. You've been wonderful for the department, for the staff and most importantly for the patients, and London's very lucky to get you.'

And because she had to do it, because it was utterly and completely the right thing to do and to have omitted it would only have raised eyebrows, as she handed him the small package Tessa leant forward and kissed him on his unshaven cheek, the bitter-sweet feeling of his skin beneath her lips, and for a lingering second his arm pulled her closer and she felt him squeeze her tight as she handed him the package.

And that was it.

It was time for Tessa to stand back and watch as he politely read the card first, the pages filled with signatures, little jokes and one-liners, all the staff wishing him well for the future. And she watched him swallow hard as he read it, knew, because she at least knew that much about him, that Max would be finding this hard.

He didn't have to feign surprise when he opened his present. A fluorescent pink pen with a large rope round it fell out first and everyone howled with laughter.

'So you don't lose it.' Tessa smiled.

His real present came next, and they shared one tiny look, both remembering that day, walking through the shop, not knowing what was to come.

When an innocent friendship had still been very much alive.

'Thanks, guys.' For a moment he gazed down at the pen set in his hands as his

Adam's apple bobbed up and down a few times.

'Look at us.' He smiled as he looked up. 'Jane in a soft neck collar, the charge nurse covered in bruises, me with one eye closed and an eyebrow full of stitches. We're worse than the patients.

'But that's what this place does to us.' He looked around the room. 'And you know the most amazing part of it all is that we come back for more. How many times do we go home and swear that's it? That we've had it up to here?' He jabbed at his neck and waited as a few murmurs of agreement made their way around the gathered audience, then Max smiled again. 'But the sun comes up the next day and we climb into our cars and head back to it, even though we swore we wouldn't, because that's what we are. Emergency staff. And that's what we'll always be. Like it or not, this place always pulls you back. It's not just the drama, though, that's keeps us here, you know that as well as I do. It's the people we work alongside day and night, the community we've built together that makes it so much more than a job to all of us.

'So with that in mind I won't keep you any longer, I'll just thank you all for coming, thank you for this wonderful present which I'll treasure and promise not to lose and say that I'll see you all next year, same time, same place. You're not getting rid of me that easily.'

The plastic cups were raised again, and Max stepped forward into the room, lost as he mingled in the crowd of colleagues. Tessa stood there, sure it was the last time she would see him, that this really was the end. Everyone would want a piece of Max to-day—the doctors' mess lunch, Admin's afternoon tea, even Narelle from the canteen had the promise of one last coffee. It was easy to slip away unnoticed to grab her bag from the changing room, tell Jane she was going to grab a few hours before the night shift started.

The hard part was pulling the curtains on the bright afternoon sun, slipping into the unmade bed where the scent of Max still lingered and trying to work out how it could all have gone so wrong.

How a wonderful friendship, a decent, kind and special man could all be reduced to this horrible pile of rubble.

CHAPTER TEN

'How come you're not at the party?' Kelly, one of the night staff, smiled curiously as Tessa joined them at the nurses' station.

'We were short.' Tessa shrugged. 'Did you hear about Kim?'

'Yes, poor thing. But surely it's a bit of overkill, filling a grad nurse's position with a charge nurse.'

Tessa gave a dismissive nod. 'Apparently I still come cheaper than an agency nurse— try working that one out.' She was hoping the conversation was over, that Kelly would just accept that she was here, but deep down Tessa knew it could never be that easy. She and Max had been friends for a long time, and the fact she wasn't at his party merited a five-minute moan at least.

'That's so unfair,' Kelly rattled on. 'You and Max are friends—surely Admin could have forgotten about the budgets for one night. You should have put your foot down. You're supposed to be off sick anyway after your adventures the other day. Max will be so disappointed if you don't go.'

Tessa doubted that. For all his bravado about a 'little talk' at the end of the day, there was no chance of that. Emily would be there, along with rest of the staff. They'd have had more privacy in the middle of the corridor! Max knew that as well as she did. He no more wanted to attempt a justification of last night's behaviour than Tessa wanted to hear it.

It had been a terrible mistake.

One never to be repeated.

'If the department's quiet around eleven, I'll take my supper break early and pop over—it's only in the doctors' mess.' Tessa forced a smile. 'I'll cut quite a dash in my uniform.'

'Well, you make sure that you do,' Kelly insisted, only dropping the painful subject when Tessa pointedly turned to the whiteboard and nodded for the late staff to start the handover.

Of course, because Tessa wanted the place to be busy, because she wanted patients hanging from the rafters and ambulances screeching into the ambulance bay, the department was quieter than the morgue. 'Go on.' Kelly nudged her as they stood listlessly cleaning the trolleys. 'You've got your pager. We'll bleep you if it gets busy. Take a good hour.'

She really didn't have much choice. Ducking into the changing rooms, Tessa splashed on a dab of perfume and a slick of lipstick, but her heart wasn't really in it. It was bad enough going to a party in your uniform, let alone the cringe factor of seeing Max's face drop a mile when she walked in.

Turning out of the entrance, Tessa lingered a moment as an ambulance pulled in. 'Go on.' Kelly shooed her off. 'It wasn't even a blue light, we'll be fine.'

But as the paramedics opened the rear doors, an awful guttural scream filled the corridor and all thoughts of parties and farewells flew from Tessa's mind as she watched the poor battered face of Josie peering out from under a swaddle of blankets as the paramedics wheeled her along.

'What happened?'

'Not sure, Tessa.' It was Ryan again and he greeted Tessa warmly, yesterday's adventure having formed an eternal bond between them.

'Found unconscious down a side street, multiple cuts and bruises. She's totally incoherent, terrified, in fact, poor old girl. All I can get is that she was at the cash machine. That's about it—the rest is just ranting. Looks like she's been mugged, there's no purse or money in her bag. We've told the police, no doubt they'll be along soon.'

'Oh, Josie.' Tessa tried to take her patient's hands but the movement only startled her and Josie jerked frantically away, screaming at the top of her voice.

'Let's get her into a cubicle,' Tessa said above the screams.

'She looks familiar,' Kelly said, her eyebrows furrowing as she tried to place the battered, bleeding face.

'Her name's Josie, she's one of the regulars. I know her pretty well, at least as much as anyone can know her. I'll deal with her.'

'But what about the party?' Kelly urged. 'We'd manage.'

'I know you would,' Tessa said, and as her eyes strayed to the pitiful sight of her patient, Tessa knew she wasn't using Josie's injuries as an excuse not to face Max. Josie needed a familiar face now and Tessa could provide it, and at the end of the day she was on duty and patients came first, always. 'But it's better if I stay.'

For the best part of an hour Tessa fought to help Josie, to clean her wounds, to get her, fighting and struggling, into a gown, all the while doing her best to orientate her, to reassure her over and over, but it all seemed to no avail. Josie had wandered off to a different scary place and for a while nothing Tessa said or did seemed to calm her.

'It's Tessa, Josie,' Tessa said gently for the hundredth time, as she wrapped a blanket around the painfully thin shoulders. At last Josie was clean and dry and the screaming seemed to have died down a touch. 'You're at the hospital, you're safe now.'

'I saw him,' Josie sobbed. 'I was at the machine and I saw him.'

'You're safe now,' Tessa said over and over until finally she seemed to be reaching Josie. 'The police will be here soon and you can tell them what happened.'

'I tried to chase him.'

'You should have just let him go,' Tessa started, but as Josie began to get agitated again Tessa realised she was on the wrong track. 'It's all OK now.'

'Where's my coat?'

'It's under the trolley, Josie. I've put it in a property bag.'

'I need my coat.'

Tessa pulled the bag out. She had already been through the coat pockets and checked the lining, but it was intact. Poor Josie had taken Tessa's advice and, Tessa thought with a huge lump in her throat, what terrible advice it had been. Suddenly the world seemed a horrible place. Josie, dear Josie who wouldn't harm a fly, who had always been safe in the little bayside town, lay on the trolley bruised and bleeding and scared, and a so-called fellow human being was to blame.

Once her wounds had been cleaned up, there wasn't much more Tessa could do, apart from stay with the old lady, reassure her over the crackling of the police walkie-talkies, guide her through the endless questions that Josie couldn't or wouldn't answer. And finally, when the interview was over, when the psychiatrist had been and a strong sedative ordered for Josie, Tessa ducked into the toilet to run the taps loudly and rant at the injustices of the world and question, as all Emergency staff did every once in a while, just why the hell they put themselves through it.

'Look who's here!' Kelly beamed as Max stood up from a stool in the annexe. 'And look at all the yummy leftovers he's brought us.'

'Hi, Max.' Tessa didn't even attempt to inject enthusiasm into her voice as she bunched up her tissue and tossed it into the wastepaper basket.

'You didn't come—' Max started.

'I had to work.'

Max nodded. 'Kelly just told me about Josie. Do you want me to put my head in?'

'She's asleep now.' Tessa shrugged. 'Anyway, she doesn't really recognise anyone.'

'Come on.' He had her hand and didn't seem to care who saw it. 'Let's go to my office.'

'No, Max.' Tessa pulled her hand away but the emergency corridor really wasn't the place for this type of conversation and after a reluctant pause Tessa marched off to his office, the empty desk and discarded boxes ramming home the fact that she'd already lost him.

'Emily and I are finished.'

'Again,' Tessa sneered.

'We have been since you went away on the trauma course, and if you'd get off your high horse for five minutes I might be able to explain things.'

'Guess what, Max?' Tessa slapped her hands on her thighs in exasperation, interrupting his flurry of words with the most abrupt of voices. 'I don't want to get off my high horse. I happen to quiet like it up here, and for your information I've got enough problems of my own to deal with without worrying about what's going on between you and Emily. Yes, we slept together and, yes, as far as sex goes it was pretty darn good, but it didn't change anything, the earth didn't move that much! You're still flying off to London tomorrow, I'm still going to be here and you're still a liar!'

'I've never lied to you, Tessa. The fact is you just don't want to hear the truth!'

'Then take the hint and leave me alone, Max.'

'I don't get you, Tess…' He was shaking his head, looking at her with utter bemusement. She could smell whisky on his breath but she knew that the alcohol hadn't touched the sides, that the raw emotion in his voice had nothing to do with too much to drink and everything to do with her. 'For all the friendly smiles, for all the cosy chats and comradeship you bang on about, you don't really let anyone within a square mile of you, do you? Why do you keep pushing me away, Tessa? Why won't you hear me out? Why won't you just let me love you?'

'Because I don't want your love, Max.' She watched as he winced, amazing even herself at the assuredness in her voice. 'So there's really nothing more to say. I just want you to go.'

'You don't mean that.'

'Yes, Max,' Tessa said slowly, deliberately, even managing to look him in the eye as she did so, 'I do mean it. I just want you to go and get on with your life, so that I can get on with mine.'

Opening the office door, she watched as Emily teetered towards them, her eyes glittering from too many tears and too much champagne, and Tessa just managed a rueful shake of her head.

'Your fiancée's here, Max.' Tessa gave him the blackest look she could muster. 'Or should I say ex? I really can't seem to keep up.'

CHAPTER ELEVEN

THE only good thing about night duty, Tessa thought as she started her car on Saturday night, was that at least she been so exhausted after her shift she'd actually managed to sleep.

Well, sort of.

Looking at the clock on the dashboard, Tessa glanced up at the sky, squinting her eyes in the late evening sky, trying to make out a flash of silver, the sight of a plane.

What was the point?

Even if she did see a plane, what were the chances of it being Max's?

Zero.

And even if it was Max's, what could she do about it?

Nothing.

It felt strange, going into the hospital with two bunches of flowers, but every now and then nurses were visitors, too.

'Hey, Josie.' Tessa handed a bunch over and Josie looked them over critically.

'They'd better take them outside at night, it's not good to sleep with flowers beside you, you know.'

'I can take them back if you like,' Tessa teased. 'They'll brighten up the nurses' station in Emergency.'

'Just leave them there.' Josie gestured to her locker. 'Rita came to see me.'

'Oh, its Rita now, is it?' Tessa grinned. 'What happened to the ''blooming social worker''?'

'She's a nice girl actually. Look at all these leaflets she gave me. Can you imagine me in a retirement village?'

Tessa looked down at the brochures, trying not to sound too enthusiastic though her heart leapt at the prospect.

'It looks lovely. Look, they've got lawn bowls and bingo, even a hairdresser's.'

'What would I need a hairdresser for?'

Tessa grinned. 'You could be a redhead again.'

'Fiercely expensive thought.'

'I guess,' Tessa sighed, putting the brochures back nonchalantly, though her heart was in her mouth.

'Still I can afford it apparently. It would be nice to have somewhere…somewhere decent. Would you come and see me? I mean, I know I'm just a patient and you must get a lot of old coots like me…'

'You're a one-off, Josie.' Tessa laughed. 'Of course I'd come and visit. Anyway, I have to go now. There's someone else I need to see before I start my shift, but I'll pop in and see you next week.'

Even though it was the hospital she worked in, Tessa felt as awkward as any visitor when she entered the gynae ward and made her way to the nurses' station.

'I was hoping to see Kim Billings, to give her these flowers from the staff in Emergency.'

'It's probably not the best time.' The ward sister smiled apologetically. 'Dr Elves has just been into see her and she's a bit upset.'

Tessa's face dropped. 'Oh.'

'The baby's all right.' Dr Elves looked up with a smile from the notes he was writing. 'I think she's just a bit overwhelmed. I just gave her a sedative, so it might be better if we let her rest for now.'

'Of course.' Tessa handed the flowers to the sister. 'Could you let her know that we're all thinking of her?'

Tessa walked off, slightly taken back when Dr Elves joined her as they waited at the lift, exchanging brief, polite smiles.

'I seem to have spent most of the day mopping up tears.' He half laughed as he punched the buttons, totally unaware of the agony his small talk was creating. 'As you no doubt know, your consultant left this afternoon. I don't know who was more upset when we waved him off, my wife or my daughter.'

'It's always hard, saying goodbye,' Tessa murmured, grateful when the lift door pinged and Dr Elves got out and she had thirty seconds of privacy as the lift descended again. Thirty seconds to acknowledge her loss, to admit he'd definitely gone, before the lift doors slid open and she faced the world.

A world without Max.

It was a busy night, but not busy enough. Everywhere Tessa turned there seemed to be bits of Max, old patients' notes filled with his appalling handwriting, one of his many stethoscopes dangling over the blood-pressure machine, even the fact her pen survived the night safely in her pocket without Max swiping it then promptly losing it.

'What can I get you, love?' Narelle smiled her gappy smile and Tessa forced one back.

'Just a coffee, thanks.'

'You need more than a coffee inside you after a full night's work. Now, I'll ask again—what can I get you?'

How she'd love to have gone off food, for the weight to fall off her as she pined away, but life wasn't always like that.

Well, not for Tessa anyway.

Visions of greeting Max thin and divine this time next year melted away as Tessa gave in in an instant. Bacon butties smothered in brown sauce would always figure large in Tessa's list of creature comforts, and today was no exception.

Great, Tessa thought as she wiped the last of the sauce with her toast. I can't even be thin when I'm pining. But, then, that was her life story.

Max, the ultimate chocolate box. She couldn't just wreck her diet with one chocolate, couldn't feel guilty over one kiss. No, she had to go right on ahead and have the whole blessed box, orange creams and all!

Sleep wouldn't come and after an entire morning spent tossing and turning and pounding her pillow, Tessa gave in and headed for the beach.

A walk might burn away a few calories, then she might not feel quite so guilty about her blow-out this morning. She could always start her diet tomorrow…

There was always tomorrow.

The beach was almost deserted, apart from the occasional dog and its master and a couple of serious fishermen standing thigh-high in their waders, Tessa had it all to herself, but she concentrated on one small area, pacing up and down along the honey-colored, soft sand, the tranquil picture-perfect scene marred by her palpable tension.

Her mind was saturated with Max, saturated. Every cell screaming out at the unfairness of it all, swinging from despair to guilt. Yet every now and then a blissful image would override her torment, a snippet to sustain her, a memory of the few hours when life had been kind and good and she'd truly believed they might make it. The heaven of his touch, the soft sweet glow of togetherness, only to be obliterated as a wave of shame obliterated her haven of peace.

How many times had Tessa dreamed about him walking towards her, how many times over the years had she closed her eyes and imagined Max smiling in the sun at her, dreamed her impossible dreams?

Watching a yellow taxi pull over, seeing Max get out, hearing his shout, his impatient wave, Tessa actually kept her face impassive, sure after so many dreams this was just another, that the sun was playing tricks on her sleep-deprived mind, that the man running towards her surely wasn't him. But as he drew closer, when the face didn't magically transform into just another guy that looked a bit like him, Tessa had to resist the urge to run, to kick up her heels and cross the beach towards him because, if dreams did come true, if her longing had somehow materialised him, there was no point in getting excited. What could Max possibly say to excuse what they had done?

'You're supposed to be in London.' It wasn't the friendliest of greetings, it didn't even begin to sum up the magnitude of the situation, but it was the best Tessa could do.

'It's cold in London.'

Tessa gave a dismissive half-smile and carried on walking, her mind refusing to acknowledge that he was really here beside her.

'I made it as far as Singapore, and I knew I had to come back. Tessa, we never did talk.'

'You could have rung,' Tessa said rudely.

'What, and listen to your answering machine again? I've tried that, about a hundred times. Do you ever listen to your messages, Tessa?'

'There was nothing worth listening to.' She turned, acknowledging him properly for the first time, her eyes flaming with anger. 'Look, I'm sorry if you've had a wasted journey, Max. I'm sorry if your grand gesture of flying back from Singapore isn't going to win you any Brownie points with me, but I really don't want to see you. I'm not putting all this on you, Max—I'm just as much to blame. I'm well over the age of consent, but what we did was wrong and all I want to do is put it behind me, to try my best to forget what happened, and hope and pray no one treats me as poorly as I've treated Emily.'

'Tessa.' Max's voice was sharp and from his stance Tessa knew he meant business. 'You're damn well going to listen to me. We did nothing wrong. Nothing,' he emphasised, as she looked at him incredulously.

'Have you ever started something?' Max ventured as Tessa hesitantly sat down on the warm golden sand and stared out to the ocean, pointedly not looking at him. 'Something that seemed liked a good idea at the time, but as soon as it's started, as soon as you've agreed, you've immediately regretted it, watched it snowball out of control, knowing that there's no turning back, that you've made the biggest mistake of your life.'

'Oh, I can think of a couple of examples.' Tessa gave a little shrug. 'Dangling off a cliff face, then remembering I'm terrified of heights. Sleeping with my boss, believing him when he said it was over between him and his fiancée...' Her eyes briefly looked up at him then flicked dismissively away. 'Then finding out the next morning he was still very much engaged.'

'It is over,' Max said emphatically.

'No, Max, it isn't over until Emily knows about it.'

'Emily does know.' Max sat down beside her. 'We finished weeks ago.' He waited for her to say something, to look at him even, but a cynical laugh was the only response he got. 'Emily wanted different things from the relationship than I did.'

'Like monogyny or fidelity perhaps.'

'You're not making this easy, Tessa.'

'I don't want it to be easy on you, Max, I don't want to hear you attempt to justify this.'

'Well, that's just tough,' he said harshly. 'Because for once in your life, Tessa, you're going to listen to me. The taxi's still there and if, after you've heard me out, you still want me to go, then I'm out of here. You have my word.'

'And we all know what that's worth,' Tessa sneered, then shook her head in disbelief, hardly able to fathom the venom in her own voice.

'We wanted different things,' Max said again, ignoring her outburst, his voice calmer now, as if the awful, bitter exchange hadn't even occurred. 'I wanted the lot—babies, white picket fences, the whole family package, but Emily...' It was Max shaking his head now. 'The only name change she wanted was a few more letters after her surname. Her career was always going to come first, last and always. She accused me of being chauvinist, but I really don't think I was. Sure, I love my career, love my work, but I love finishing my shift, Tessa, I love my time away from the hospital. Anyway, we both finally realised that it just wasn't going to happen for us, that we were just too different, and I guess we didn't love each other enough to compromise.'

'So why didn't you just break up, Max?' Tessa's face was contorted with anger, tears held well back as she struggled with what he was telling her. 'Why is Emily still wearing your ring, talking about your weekends at the beach and romantic dinners for two? Answer me that, Max.'

'Because she wanted everyone to believe that we're still together.' He watched as

Tessa swallowed hard, watched her pained, angry eyes finally turn to him. 'She didn't want to deal with the gossip while this promotion was in the air, she thought it might affect her chances if the powers that be thought she was having personal problems.'

'There would have been gossip, Tess,' Max implored.

She nodded slowly, her eyebrows furrowing as his words sank in.

'And lots of it. But if one of us left, headed off to do a course or a six-month rotation somewhere, we could let people think it just fizzled out, somehow avoid all the sympathetic stares and nudges, and when Emily suggested it, it made sense.'

'If it was her idea, why didn't she go?' Tessa bit back nastily.

'She's just about to make consultant, Tessa. She's worked herself into the ground building up her reputation here, proving she was as good if not better than any man...'

'So you offered to go?'

He gave a tiny shrug. 'My résumé could use a bit of livening up, and at the time it didn't seem such a big deal—take a year off, see a bit of the world, come back twelve months later and pick up where I left off...'

'But why all the secrecy, Max?' Tessa interrupted. 'Why couldn't you just tell Emily about us, tell her how you were feeling. Surely she would have understood?'

'Tessa.' Max turned, his face inches away, his eyes boring into her. 'Listen to me, this is important. We've been friends for five years now, yes?'

She simply nodded. The maths in her head had been done long ago.

'And for those five years, I promise, as true as I'm sitting here, that friends were all that we were. Sure, I thought you were great, gorgeous, funny—take your pick—and there was no doubt in my mind that one day very soon some lucky guy was going to snap you up. It just never, not once, entered my head that it might be me.

'For the last two years I've been in a relationship, doing my best to make things work with Emily, not imagining how it would be with another woman. But after we broke up...' He let out a long ragged sigh, ran a slightly shaking hand over his unshaven chin. 'You went off on that trauma course and all I did was miss you. You, Tessa, not the charge nurse, not my brunch buddy, you, Tessa, and the way you make me laugh, the way you make me feel. It hit me like a thunderbolt. How could I tell Emily? How could I ask her to believe that there had never been anything between you and I, that I hadn't been unfaithful? I know the truth, Tessa, and even I have trouble believing it could all be so innocent.'

He grinned then screwed his eyes closed as what looked strangely like a blush darkened his cheeks. 'I'm not really up on the latest chat up-lines. You must have wondered what on earth was going on.'

'Just a bit,' Tessa agreed, a reluctant smile wobbling on her full mouth.

'I haven't chatted anyone up for years, hell, I haven't been on a first date for what seemed like half a century, and I didn't have a clue how to go about it, let alone to tell you how I was feeling. There I was disappearing, for a year, and like a fool I was hoping to walk back in where I'd left things, suddenly single and free to ask you out. But I'm not that special, Tessa...'

A cool breeze was coming off the ocean and Tessa hugged her knees to her chest, taking in all Max was telling her, her mind working fast, reliving the last few weeks, and finally the missing pieces of the jigsaw slotted into place. Emily's sudden intimate declarations made sense now, her desperate attempts to affirm to her colleagues that she and Max were most definitely a couple. Her tears during Kim's ultrasound made sense now, too—they hadn't been the tears of a lover left behind but a woman struggling with the end of her relationship, and maybe dealing with the fact that babies wouldn't ever be on her agenda.

'You're a beautiful woman, Tessa, and you can deny that as much as you like but that's what you are, a beautiful woman who deserves to be loved. You weren't going to wait around for a guy you didn't even know loved you.'

'Why not? I've already waited five years.' Her dark serious eyes looked up at him. Honesty just a breath away. 'I've loved you for five years, Max.' The tears that normally poured so readily from her eyes were staying away now, so determined was Tessa that her moment of truth would be spoken in a clear voice, that Max absolutely understood what she was saying. 'That's why I feel so bad. It didn't suddenly just happen, not for me anyway. I've been longing for this, dreaming of this, and in some way I feel I must have engineered it, that I'm to blame for your break-up.'

'No.'

Tessa watched, startled, as she realised it was Max, not her, that was crying, that for once she was the one being strong.

'It isn't your fault and it isn't mine. Emily and I just didn't love each other enough, and we both know that now.'

'I saw her father yesterday.' Tessa was almost shouting. 'He told me that she's devastated. That she didn't want you to go.'

'Because she realised she'd made a mistake!' Max's voice overrode Tessa's, his eyes imploring her to listen, to believe. 'Emily knew she'd overreacted. She's not going to miss out on promotion because of a bit of a gossip and the hospital isn't going to grind to a halt because we've broken up—we're not that important! Sure, our parents will be upset when they find out and there'll be a ton of gossip, but we would have survived it. But I can't survive this, Tessa, I can't fly to the other side of the world without you knowing the truth. And I can't bear the fact that you don't trust me.'

'I want to trust you,' Tessa sobbed. 'And I so badly wanted to believe that we weren't doing anything wrong, but I'm scared of making a mistake, scared of ending up like…' The words strangled in her throat, and she shook her head in anguish at her failure to finish, pushing the palms of her hands into her eyes in a futile attempt to collect her breath.

'Like your parents.'

Pain ripped through him as he watched her tiny nod, heard her intake of breath as she fought back nineteen years' worth of tears and pain.

'We're nothing like them, Tessa, nor will we ever be.'

'You don't know that.' Her face was still buried in her hands, like a child blocking out the world, and Max gently gripped her wrists, pulling her hands down and placing a gentle thumb on her chin, dragging her eyes to meet his.

'I do know that. Because I love you, Tessa, and I'm actually starting to believe that you love me, too, and if we're going to do this, we're going to make damn sure that we do it right.'

His lips found hers then, rough and urgent as if the strength and depth of his passion could somehow cast away the last doubts clouding her mind,

The taxi beeped and they both looked up, startled at the intrusion, the ticking meter forcing them to a conclusion.

'He can wait,' Max said quickly.

'It must be costing you a fortune.'

Max shrugged. 'You should have seen what they charged for the air ticket. It's turning into the most expensive first date in history.'

Tessa smiled but it wobbled at the edges. 'Especially when you're not even going to get asked in for coffee.' She watched as despair flooded his eyes, as he opened his mouth to argue then closed it again as Tessa tentatively continued.

'You have to go to London, Max. You have to finish what you've started. I can see Emily's point, I can see how hard it would be to ride out the gossip and if you come back, if you and I are suddenly on together, no one's going to believe it just happened....'

'We know the truth, that's what's important.'

'No, Max.' Tessa shook her head, brushing the tears that streaked her face with the back of her hand. 'This isn't just about us, it touches too many people.' Tessa scuffed at the sand with her toes, a plan forming in her mind so clear, so concise it surely must have always been there. 'I've been through a lot recently—the inquest, the rescue. My mum was just telling me I need to get away, take a break.' Tessa gave a small shrug. 'Maybe she was right. Who knows? Six months from now I might just pack up my backpack and head off to Europe. I might even look up my old friend Max Slater and see if there's a job going in his hospital. Two Aussies far away from home, one getting over his engagement break-up, well, there's no telling what might happen...'

She was sobbing now, sobbing at the thought of finding him only to lose him so soon, but her tears were tempered with joy, her conscience shining clear, and Tessa knew that, as hard as her decision had been, it was the right one.

'You'd come to London? But, Tessa, you love it here...'

'I love you Max. It was only a dream job when I was working alongside you. I want to do things the right way. I know now that we've done nothing wrong, but Emily doesn't deserve to be hurt any more than she has been and we don't deserve to start our relationship as the bad guys with all the gossip and finger-pointing that would come with it. What you said before, Max, was true—if we're going to do this then we're going to do it right, and that starts here.'

Her decision made Tessa stood up quickly, scared she might waver, scared at how easy it would be to wave the taxi off and ride the storm together.

'You'll come to the airport?' Max voice was startled, stunned at the haste in her decision, her desire to get moving.

'Do you really have to ask?'

'It might be a while before I can get a flight.'

They were walking towards the taxi, their hands entwined, lingering a last moment on the beach together as they contemplated six months apart.

'I hope so.' An impish grin spread over her face. 'And if we're going for a record in expensive first dates, we might as well break it in style. Surely there must be a hotel at the airport.'

As Max started to laugh Tessa realised how much she had missed that sound, how she hadn't heard him laughing for so long now.

'Come on, then.' He dropped her hand and turned with a smile. 'With that incentive I'll race you to the taxi.'

'You always win,' Tessa grumbled as she joined him, panting and breathless, at the taxi.

'I always do, don't I?' Max beamed, wrapping her in the warmest of embraces, planting butterfly kisses along her soft cheeks. 'And you, Tessa Hardy, are the best prize of all.'

EPILOGUE

HEATHROW airport was huge! It was a city in itself and Tessa tried her best not to look like the small-town girl she was, to push her trolley along the green taped line with an air of superiority, to look as nonchalant and sophisticated as the rest of the undoubted frequent flyers, as if she, too, did this sort of thing every day.

Her resolve didn't last.

Suddenly she was through customs, turning a corner and surveying the throng of people leaning over the barriers with hungry eyes until the one face she wanted to see came into focus. All thoughts of sophistication evaporated as Tessa pushed her unwilling trolley at breakneck speed, clipping a few ankles as she ran to the outstretched arms of Max, eternally grateful for the tiny toothbrush and paste the airline had provided as Max kissed her, oblivious of the hold-up they were causing, blissfully unaware of the tuts and shaking heads as trolleys diverged around them and Security edged a bit closer.

'I think we'd better get out of here.' Max laughed, his arm draped possessively around her, pushing her loaded trolley with one hand as he nuzzled her neck, neither able to believe after all this time they were finally reunited.

'Talk fast,' Max warned as he slipped into the driver's seat, 'because once we get to the flat the talking's over. How was the flight?'

'Fantastic!' Tessa enthused, her hand on his thigh as they negotiated the exit barriers.

'You're supposed to say it was awful, that you're exhausted and you're never setting foot on a plane again.'

'But it was great and the food was just wonderful.' Tessa rummaged in her handbag. 'I kept all the menus.'

'You're crazy.'

Everything seemed huge. The motorways had more lanes than Tessa could count, even the cars went faster here!

'How are Kim and the baby?'

'Great. He's...' Her voice trailed off for a second. 'He's perfect.'

'You're not getting all clucky, are you?'

Tessa laughed, really laughed. 'Actually, no.' She pulled a picture out of her bag and flashed it briefly at Max.

'Oh, dear!'

'Exactly.' Tessa giggled. 'She thinks he's the most beautiful baby in the world and the funniest part of it was when her husband Mark walked in—the baby's an absolute dead ringer!'

It was the sort of conversation you could only have with your closest friend and Tessa instantly felt herself relax. They *were* still friends; lovers, yes, partners, yes, but always friends.

'Ours will be gorgeous,' Max said easily as Tessa cheeks burned with his natural presumption. Could it all be so easy? Could she, Tessa, really have it all?

'I had a drink with Emily on Friday.' Perhaps it wasn't the most romantic of things Tessa could have said, but she wanted it out of the way, wanted the air cleared before they got home.

Home. She hadn't even seen it. By all accounts it was a tiny, phenomenally expensive bedsit, but apparently it had a bed and a kettle and, more importantly, it had Max.

So it *was* home.

'How is she?'

'Deliriously happy. The wedding's only a few weeks away now and she's busy organising the whole town with military precision. You know how laid-back Fred is, he just agrees to everything...'

'And she's honestly happy,' Max checked, then shook his head ruefully. 'I must be the only guy on earth who's actually pleased that his ex-fiancée and future wife went out for a drink and got on so well.' He turned sharply at her intake of breath. 'What? What did I say?'

'Nothing,' Tessa mumbled, sinking down in her seat and watching the world rush past the outside lane.

'Come on, Tessa, don't go all quiet on me.'

Tessa nibbled her thumbnail for a moment, her eyes still trained on the world outside the car. 'You don't have to marry me. I didn't come expecting you to propose or anything, we haven't even gone out on a proper date yet.'

'Tess.' Max looked over very quickly then turned back to the road. 'Can I call you that now?'

She could hear him laughing at her and gave a very grudging nod.

'I didn't drag you to the other side of the world for a couple of cheap meals and a night at the movies. I know what films you like, I know what your favourite dishes on the menu would be, we're past all that, Tess, way past it.'

'I know,' Tessa muttered, feeling silly yet pleased all the same.

'And if you won't agree to marry me, I'll just refuse to sleep with you until you give in.'

'Oh, and you're such a fabulous lover that I'll relent in two minutes flat,' Tessa bit back sarcastically.

'You know I am.' His hand had moved from the gear lever and dragged her hand back to his thigh. 'So what's it to be?'

'I'll let you know when we get there.'

It *was* a tiny bedsit.

Tiny.

'Well, there's the bed,' Tessa joked. 'Where are we supposed to sit?'

'We don't. It's the bed or nothing—terrible shame, that. We're on the flightpath, by the way, so if you think the earth is moving for you around five a.m. don't automatically assume that it's me!'

As great the flight had been, Tessa needed a shower more than she needed the coffee Max was making, and as she peeled off her clothes Tessa looked at the marks her jeans had left on her waist and legs and her impossibly swollen ankles, courtesy of twenty-four hours on a plane, and wondered how Max could truly want her.

Her doubt lasted about two seconds flat as she stepped out of the shower and into his arms.

'My ankles are swollen.'

'You need to elevate them,' Max said with a wink.

'I'd love to,' Tessa quipped back, 'but you're on a sex strike, remember?'

'Only till you agree to marry me.'

Tessa looked down. 'Well, they really are very swollen and I do really need to lie down.' She looked up. Max was gazing at her, utter love and adoration blazing from his eyes, and Tessa knew then that dreams did come true.

Sometimes you could have it all.

'You're gorgeous, you know that?' Max said, pulling her down onto the bed beside him, his hands cupping her warm breasts still damp from the shower, his lips brushing her fragrant skin as he worked his way along her neck. 'Absolutely gorgeous.'

'Keep telling me, Max,' Tessa sighed, melting at his touch, the roaring sound of a jet plane taking off fading to a distant droan as they disappeared into their own private place. 'I'm actually starting to believe it.'

MEDICAL ROMANCE™

Large Print

Titles for the next three months...

April

THE BABY BONDING — Caroline Anderson
IN-FLIGHT EMERGENCY — Abigail Gordon
THE DOCTOR'S SECRET BABY — Judy Campbell
THE ITALIAN DOCTOR'S PROPOSAL — Kate Hardy

May

OUTBACK ENGAGEMENT — Meredith Webber
THE PLAYBOY CONSULTANT — Maggie Kingsley
THE BABY EMERGENCY — Carol Marinelli
THE DOCTOR'S CHRISTMAS GIFT — Jennifer Taylor

June

FOR CHRISTMAS, FOR ALWAYS — Caroline Anderson
CONSULTANT IN CRISIS — Alison Roberts
A VERY SPECIAL CHRISTMAS — Jessica Matthews
THE ITALIAN'S PASSIONATE PROPOSAL — Sarah Morgan

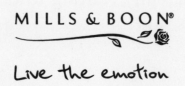

MILLS & BOON®

Live the emotion

0304 LP 1P Medical